S0-AEB-775

A QUIET STRENGTH

THE SUSANNA RUTH KREHBIEL STORY

by Amelia Mueller

Faith and Life Press
Newton, Kansas

i

Copyright © 1992 by Faith and Life Press, Newton, Kansas 67114-0347.
This publication may not be reproduced, stored in a retrieval system, or trans-
mitted in whole or in part, in any form by any means, electronic, mechanical,
photocopying, recording, or otherwise without prior permission of Faith and
Life Press.

Printed on recycled paper in the United States of America
98 97 96 95 94 93 92 7 6 5 4 3 2 1

Library of Congress Number 92-082738
International Standard Book Number 0-87303-201-2

Editorial direction for Faith and Life Press by Susan E. Janzen; copyediting by
Edna Dyck; design by John Hiebert; cover art by Kristin Ediger Goering; printing
by Mennonite Press.

PREFACE

This book is historical fiction in that the conversations and some other details are fictitious. However, it is based as accurately as possible on the following documents:

1. Susanna Amalia Krehbiel's autobiography, written by Susanna A. Krehbiel in 1911, and later translated into English.

2. "A Travel Sketch from the Middle of the Past Century," written in German by J.E. Ruth and published in installments in several issues of *Der Herold,* beginning with the January 6, 1910, issue. Translated by Amelia Mueller.

3. "History of the Ruth Family," a literal translation by Jacob E. Ruth of the history written in German by his father, David Ruth (Father in the story in this book). Printed in the Ruth genealogy, *The Ruth Families* (Fountain Press, 1981) compiled by Warren E. Kriebel, Souderton, Pennsylvania.

4. Information about the births, deaths, etc., of members of the Ruth and Dahlem families, found in the above Ruth genealogy.

5. The original Packetboat Passage Agreement, still in the possession of Lois and Walter Lehman of Halstead, Kansas, descendants of Barbara Ruth. Translated by Amelia Mueller.

6. *Prairie Pioneer* by Christian Krehbiel, published in 1961 by Faith and Life Press, Newton, Kansas.

7. *History of the Mennonite General Conference* by H.P. Krehbiel, published by the author in 1898.

8. *An Introduction to Mennonite History* Cornelius J. Dyck, editor, published by Herald Press, Scottdale, Pennsylvania, 1967.

Although the group of Mennonites who came over from Eichstock and other parts of South Germany in the 1840s and 1850s and settled in the West Point, Iowa, and Summerfield, Illinois, area, was small, they played an important part in the beginning of the General Conference Mennonite Church. In the section "A General Conference Is Born" of *An Introduction to Mennonite History*, edited by Cornelius J. Dyck, the statement is made: "The initiative toward union came from the congregations at West Point, Iowa."

Susanna's autobiography and her husband Christian Krehbiel's book, *Prairie Pioneer*, tell about the important role played by Christian and Susanna in the immigration and settling of the Mennonites from Russia, Volhynia, Polish Russia, and northern Germany in the United States in the 1870s, and their becoming a part of the General Conference Mennonite Church.

INTRODUCTION

Susanna Ruth Krehbiel sat quietly in her chair, looking at the paper on the table in front of her. Yesterday evening she and her son, Jacob, had talked for hours, remembering things that had happened in the past.

"You should write down some of these things you have told me," Jacob had said. "There is so much that happened in your life that your children and grandchildren and great grandchildren will want to know."

This morning he had brought her a pen and some paper.

"Today would be a good time to begin writing the story of your life," he had said with a smile.

"I hardly know where to begin," she had responded, and Jacob had answered with a mischievous grin, "Begin at the beginning." Then he had given her a loving pat on the shoulder and walked out of the room.

"The story of my life?" Susanna said out loud to herself. "Write the story of my life?"

She let her mind wander back through the years. Her life had been a full, busy one, not always happy, and certainly not easy much of the time. But now, in retrospect, she realized that it had been a good life in many ways.

She thought about her husband, Christian, and his work as a traveling minister for so many years, how much he had done to help the Mennonites from Russia, Prussia, and Polish

Russia to come to the United States to begin a new life; of his interest in, and work with the Indians in Kansas and Oklahoma; his concern for the orphans, for whom he had provided a home for many years.

Christian had done all of this. But he had not done it alone. She, Susanna, had always tried to help in every way that she could. Christian's busy and meaningful life had been her life also.

"Begin at the beginning," Jacob had said.

With a smile on her face, Susanna began to write: "Today, the 9th of January, 1911, I, Susanna Amelia Krehbiel, nee Ruth, wish to begin a sort of autobiography for my dear children. . . ."

CHAPTER 1

"Come now, children," Susanna could hear Mother calling. "It's time to start to school."

Susanna Ruth walked slowly out of the bedroom where she had gone to put on her bonnet. On the outside she was ready to go to school. But inside, in the way she felt, she did not think that she would ever be ready.

She envied four-year-old Barbara, who was still sleeping in the bed she shared with Susanna in the girls' room, and two-year-old David, who was toddling around the house in his nightshirt waiting for Mother to help him dress.

Until Baby Katharina was born, David had always still been fast asleep in the trundle bed in Mother and Father's bedroom when Johannes and Susanna left for school. But now that he shared a bed with his big brother Johannes, he often woke up when Mother awakened Johannes.

Ever since Susanna had started to school for the first time a few weeks before, it had been the same—that fearful feeling when it was time to leave for school. The feeling grew worse the nearer she got to school, until by the time she was sitting on her school bench she felt almost sick.

The feeling did not go away until she had walked out of the schoolhouse door at noon to start home. Then suddenly she would feel happy and free. And what fun it was to walk and run and skip and laugh and talk with Johannes, the cousins, and the friends who were walking the same way.

Johannes did not seem to be unhappy or fearful about going to school. Perhaps that was because he was two years older than Susanna and had already gone to school for two years before Susanna started. Or, perhaps it was because he was a boy. He did not seem to be afraid of Herr Nestler, the school teacher, as Susanna was—although he never did try to defy the schoolmaster by playing pranks on him as some of the bigger boys did.

Mother took Susanna's hands in her left hand and Johannes's hands in her right hand. Then she bowed her head and prayed, "Jesus in my heart, Christ in my mind, in God's name I go on my way. Amen."

Then she walked with them to the *hof* (farmyard) gate, where their cousins Katherine and Jakob were already waiting.

Eichstock, where the Ruth families lived, could not be found on any map. It wasn't a town, or even a village. It was simply a farmstead in the Germanic state of Bavaria.

At that time, the 1840s, Germany was not yet a united country. Instead, there were a number of Germanic states, each with its own government. For centuries the land in these states had been owned by noblemen who hired day laborers to do the work in their fields.

By the 1800s this had begun to change. Noblemen began to sell much of their land to individual farmers. The Palatinate, one of these Germanic states, is where the parents of Susanna's father, David Ruth, and the parents of her mother, Katharina Strohm, grew up. Mennonites here were not allowed to own land. But for many years they had been given lifelong leases that could be passed on to their children.

However, over the years, the population of the Palatinate had grown so much that good farmland had become scarce. In the neighboring state of Bavaria, the noblemen had just begun to sell some of their land, and Mennonites were allowed to own it. So many of the young Mennonites had moved to Bavaria.

Both of Susanna's grandparents—her father's parents, Gerhard and Elisabeth Rupp Ruth, and her mother's parents,

2

Pastor John Strohm and his wife—had made the move. The Strohms had settled at the Schweig, and the Ruths at nearby Eichstock.

So Father had grown up at Eichstock. Now he, David Ruth, and his brother, Johannes Ruth, and their families lived there, after buying the property from their father. The two homes in which the families lived were built together like one large house, so the children in the two families were almost like one family of brothers and sisters.

The farm buildings were built in a square, with the house and a shed for the wagons on one side, and the other farm buildings—the cow barn, the hay shed, granary, chicken house, hog shed, and machine shed—on the other three sides, forming a solid wall around the yard.

Connecting the house and the wagon and carriage shed was a large arched gateway with a heavy iron gate that could be locked at night for safety.

About a quarter of a mile from their home the children walked past the Eichstock Mennonite Church.

Susanna loved this little church where their whole family and Uncle and Aunt and all of the cousins and friends went each Sunday morning for worship, and sometimes for other meetings on weekdays as well.

And she never tired of hearing Father tell about the building and dedication of the church in 1841. It was almost the same age as Susanna. Grandfather Strohm, Mother's father, had been the first minister. He had retired before Susanna was old enough to go to church, so she had never heard him preach. Now Father was the minister, and Susanna liked to listen to him as he stood up in the high pulpit and talked to the people.

About a half mile past the church, near Schwabhausen, the way led through the Waspelhof where the Krehbiels lived. The Krehbiel and Ruth families were close friends and visited back and forth together. The children often played together outside of school hours. They were the only Mennonite children who walked the same way to school.

Jacob, the oldest of the Krehbiel boys, was seventeen,

so he no longer went to school. Christian, who was fourteen, was one of the oldest boys in school, and his sister Katharine was one of the oldest girls. Daniel Krehbiel was a little older than Susanna's brother Johannes, and Maria Krehbiel was a little older than Susanna. The two Barbaras—Barbara Ruth and Barbara Krehbiel—were almost the same age.

The two little Krehbiel boys, John and Valentine, were both a little older than Susanna's brother David.

Bavaria was Catholic, so all of the state schools were Catholic. Only Catholic children could attend them. The few Mennonite families living in the Eichstock area could not afford to have a school of their own, so the Mennonite children attended the Lutheran school in Lansenried.

As they left the Waspelhof, Christian Krehbiel said, as he did almost every morning, "Now we must walk fast so that we will not be late to school!"

Susanna did not mind that the older children walked so fast. If she concentrated on keeping up with them, she would not think so much about what things would be like when she got to school. And she didn't mind that the way was so long, especially not now in the golden, sunny springtime.

The air was soft and pleasantly warm on her face. The fruit trees that lined the narrow country road along which they walked were filled with blossoms, and wild flowers were beginning to peek through the greening grass of the meadow. Faint touches of color in the black of the freshly worked fields marked the places where the recently sown grain had already started to come up.

On the way to school the older children did not laugh and joke as they would on the way home, especially not today. This was a Monday morning.

Although Herr Nestler had classes in reading, writing, arithmetic, drawing, singing, and a little geography, he thought that the most important thing was memory work.

Every day he gave the children, even the younger ones, a poem, a Bible verse, or a quotation to learn. At the Sunday school on Sunday afternoons long passages from the Gospels and Epistles were assigned, and these had to be recited on

Monday morning. The boys and girls helped each other study the memory work on the way to school.

Fortunately, memorizing was easy for Susanna, and Mother and Father were patient about helping with the memory work. She already knew her verses as she did every Monday morning. She had never yet felt the hickory switch as some of the boys who did not know their verses had. But the fear of it was always there.

As usual on Monday morning, the first thing Herr Nestler called for was recitation of the memory work. Susanna's was one of the first to be called. Trembling so hard that she found it difficult to stand, she began to recite her verses. To her great relief she remembered every word.

One of the older boys was not so fortunate. He said part of his verses wrong, and Herr Nestler corrected him sharply. A little later, when he faltered and did not seem to know what words came next, the hickory switch descended onto his shoulders and back.

Then Herr Nestler ordered him to come to the front of the room.

"Laugh at him!" he commanded the rest of the boys and girls. "Make fun of the stupid dunce who cannot even recite his verses!"

Most of the older boys and girls did begin to jeer and make fun of the boy. Susanna looked down at her desk. She felt sorry for the boy, and she did not want to laugh at him. She never did laugh and jeer when Herr Nestler asked them to do so. But she was always afraid that Herr Nestler would punish her for not doing what he had told her to do.

During the singing lesson, which came next, Susanna relaxed. She loved to sing, and she enjoyed the singing time more than any other part of the day.

Today, as he did every Monday, Herr Nestler had a new song for them to learn. Each of the children turned to a blank page in their song books. Susanna and the other younger children sat with the older students so they could copy what they wrote.

Then Herr Nestler began to dictate the words of the

song so the older children could write them into their books. Later they would memorize the words, but when the song was new Herr Nestler allowed them to read the words.

When all of the words had been written into the books, Herr Nestler got out his violin and began to play the melody. He played and sang the song over and over until the children could sing the song with him. Then they sang some of the older songs that they all knew. But all too soon for Susanna the singing lesson was over and it was time for the reading lesson.

Susanna had found it easy to learn the sounds of the letters and to read the new words Herr Nestler taught the first-year students every day. Mother and Father had read to Susanna and her brothers so often that she thought of reading as a pleasant thing to do. The reading lesson was always over too fast to suit her. She enjoyed listening to the older children read out loud while she worked on her writing lesson.

When the older boys and girls had finished their reading lessons, Herr Nestler announced that it was time to go home.

"And remember," he told all of them, "tomorrow our month of spring vacation begins. So you will not come back here again until after that."

When school started again after the spring vacation, Susanna had a happy surprise. The school authorities had dismissed Herr Nestler and had hired another teacher, Herr Henry Fugger from Stuttgart, to take his place.

The new teacher shook hands with the children and smiled at them when they entered the schoolroom. Susanna could tell he was a kind, gentle man like Father. And there were no hickory sticks in sight.

Herr Fugger seemed to know how to make school interesting and challenging. And he had so many new and fascinating things for them to learn. Susanna even found herself enjoying memory work, because she was no longer afraid that she might forget part of what she had learned and be punished.

The pleasant school days passed quickly. Before Susanna realized it, the school year was over and it was time for spring vacation again.

Spring vacation, the beginning of a new school year,

and then the summer vacation also went by quickly. Little changed except that now cousin Daniel was going to school, too. And Christian Krehbiel and some of the other older boys were old enough that they no longer had to go to school.

Susanna found herself enjoying school more each year. Herr Fugger continued to find interesting things for them to learn. Susanna especially liked reading books about the history of Bavaria, the Palatinate, and the other Germanic states. There were interesting accounts about other countries, too, even faraway America.

The wonderland of America had been a dream for the Ruth children ever since Uncle Jakob Leisy and Aunt Leisy had been there.

Aunt Leisy was Mother's sister. The Leisys had no children, and Uncle Leisy had enough money so they had been to America several times. They had even lived there for awhile and had traveled to various parts of the United States.

After the Leisys had come back to Bavaria, the Ruth children had listened eagerly to all of the interesting things that Aunt and Uncle told them that they had seen and done.

What Susanna remembered most vividly was Aunt Leisy saying that in America one could have so many hens that one had to gather the eggs in a basket. And, she said that in America one did not have to herd the cattle!

Susanna had a good reason for remembering what Aunt had said about not having to herd the cattle.

Father and Mother both believed that children learned best by having-good examples to follow. They also encouraged their children to do things themselves as soon as they were able. So ever since she could remember, Susanna had always had some chores to do during vacation time and after school. So did Johannes and Barbara, and as soon as each was old enough, the younger children would, too.

Father had begun to suffer with rheumatism, so he was happy when Johannes was old enough to help in the field. Then, Johannes passed on to Susanna his job of watching the cows in the meadow. Barbara was the one who helped with the laundry and cleaning the house and other household chores.

Susanna liked being outdoors where she had a chance to watch some of the work that Father and Johannes did together. One of the things she noticed was that Father did not begin any activity of any importance without first asking God's help.

In the spring, when it was time to do the sowing, Father showed Johannes how to do it. After both of them had their bags of grain hung around their shoulders, Father said, "Now let us begin in God's name." Then he prayed a short prayer before they began the work.

In late summer, they hitched the team to the new reaper. Johannes held the lines to guide the horses and Father stood on the machine with the rake in his hand to rake off the grain. Father said, "Now let us drive in God's name," and thanked God for the crop they were about to harvest.

When it was time to thresh the grain with the new threshing machine Father and nine of the other Eichstock families had ordered from America, Johannes also got to help Father with that work.

"Guiding the horses for the reaper or helping with the threshing would be fun," Susanna thought as she went to let the cows out of the barn to take them to the meadow.

Watching the cows was definitely not fun! Susanna had decided that on the first day she had to do it.

The Ruth cows were not the only ones grazing in the meadow. There were no fences or hedges or barriers of any kind to keep the cows where they were supposed to graze. Father had told Susanna that her job was to keep their cows from straying to places they were not supposed to go. She could visit with the other young cowherds or even play games with them, but she must never, never forget to keep an eye on the cows or to let them walk out of the meadow.

On that first day Susanna had discovered that some of the cows did not want to stay where they were supposed to graze. There always seemed to be at least one of them that wanted to go somewhere else! Even when all of them were where they were supposed to be, Susanna found that she could not relax.

8

Whenever one of the cows did start to stray, Susanna was filled with a thousand anxieties that the cow would get so far away that Susanna could not bring her back.

Susanna knew that Father would not punish or scold her if that happened. He was always loving and gentle with his children, never cross or angry. But Susanna did not want to see the disappointed look she had sometimes seen in his eyes when one of the children disobeyed him or did not measure up to his expectations.

"I wish David was big enough that it would be his job to watch the cows," she found herself thinking every day. "Or better still, that we lived in a place where one did not need to herd them at all."

Chapter 2

The year Susanna was ten, everything in her life seemed suddenly to change. It all began when Mr. Krehbiel decided to sell his farm at Kleinschwabhausen and move to America.

"Actually," Father told the rest of the family as they sat around the table eating the noon meal, "this is not a sudden decision. He has been thinking about it for some time, especially since Jakob was drafted into the Bavarian army. Fortunately, Bavaria allows us Mennonites who have conscientious objections to having our sons fight in wars, to buy their freedom, and Mr. Krehbiel did this for his oldest son. But he had to borrow the money to do it, and since he has five more sons, he knows that he could not do that for all of them.

"In America there is no military draft as there is here in Germany, is there?" Mother asked thoughtfully.

She was looking at Johannes as she said it, and Susanna knew what she was thinking. It would be only a few years before Johannes would be old enough and Father would face the same problem that Mr. Krehbiel had now. Susanna knew that Father did not believe in violence of any kind.

"A follower of Christ should act in love toward all people at all times," she had heard him say many times. "And having our government train our young men to kill somebody in battle would be contrary to Christ's will for his followers."

So Father would not want Johannes or the younger boys to go into the army either. Would he have enough money to buy their freedom when the time came for them to be drafted into military service, or would he have to borrow it, too?

The Krehbiels left for America in May, and their going left a big empty spot for the Ruth families. A day had seldom gone by without the three families having some contact with each other.

It seemed strange not to be able to stop in at the Waspèlhof on the way to school and have the Krehbiel children walk the rest of the way with them. In the evening at home the conversation always centered around the Krehbiel's trip, with Mother hoping that they were having a safe, pleasant voyage, and Father wondering where Mr. Krehbiel would decide to buy land, and both of them hoping that it would not be too long before a letter would arrive from across the waters.

But before the letter arrived, something else happened that began to change life even more for the Ruth families than having the Krehbiels leave Bavaria.

Uncle Leisy also sold his farm and made plans to emigrate to America!

But the Leisys decided they did not want to go alone. They knew that ever since the changes in the government of Bavaria in 1848, a number of Mennonites were concerned. Bavaria was a Catholic country, and even though there had been no persecution or discrimination, some of the Mennonites had been worried about what might happen.

The Leisys decided to wait until the next spring to emigrate. They thought that perhaps by then other friends and relatives might be ready to go along. In the meantime, Uncle and Aunt would live with Mother and Aunt Leisy's brother, Henry Strohm, at the Schweig.

One day in the fall, after Uncle and Aunt Leisy had spent some time in the Mannheim area, they came to Eichstock to visit the Ruths and some other families.

In the afternoon, Uncle Leisy, Father, and Uncle John went for a walk in the fields, and then before Leisys left, the men talked for a long time in the barnyard.

That evening at supper Father was so lost in thought that he had little to say. There were questions in Mother's eyes, but she did not ask them out loud. Even the younger children seemed to realize that there had been something important about Uncle's visit that Father had to think about, and there was little of the usual childish chatter at the table.

As soon as the meal was over, Father took the little ones to their room to help them get ready for bed as he usually did, and Susanna could hear him answering their questions about Uncle Leisy and America. By the time he came back into the room, Mother, Susanna, and Barbara had finished washing the dishes and everyone had settled down for their evening tasks.

Barbara and David were busy with homework, Johannes was reading, and Mother and Susanna were knitting.

Mother pulled out a chair for Father to sit down.

"What is it?" she asked him. "What did Uncle Leisy have to say that makes you so lost in your thoughts tonight?"

"Well," Father answered slowly, "as you know, Leisy is trying to get a group together to go with them when they go back to America. A number of families and young people in the Mannheim area are interested in going. And now he came to Eichstock to find out whether some of us will also want to go along. He talked to brother Johannes and me about that. As you know, this is not the first time he has tried to persuade us."

"Yes," Mother answered, "My sister has been talking to me about it, too." Then she asked softly, "And what answer did you give him?"

Instead of answering her question, Father said, "What he reported about the friends in Mannheim in the Palatinate made my mind go back to so many things in the past. I was thinking about our forefathers fleeing from Switzerland because they were being persecuted there. They settled in the Palatinate mainly because their religious beliefs were tolerated there, but also because the princes who owned the huge stretches of land that had been devastated by the Thirty Years' War were willing to let those religious refugees farm pieces of their land under a hereditary lease."

Mother nodded. "But our parents left the Palatinate as young people and came here to Bavaria because by that time there was no longer enough land in the Palatinate available for the young people who were ready to start farming on their own," she said. "And we can thank them for it. Life has been good for us here."

"Yes," Father agreed quickly. "That is certainly true. But now land is becoming scarce here in Bavaria, too. And then there is always the problem of the military draft."

He looked around at the group seated at the table. Then he added softly, "I have been thinking about this prayerfully ever since Leisy left, and I have decided that we should go."

Mother nodded as though she had expected something like this. Johannes and David and Susanna and Barbara just looked at each other. They were speechless.

"We? Go to America?" the surprised expression on each face asked.

"Uncle's plans do not give us much time to decide or get ready," Father went on. "The journey will take several months, so he wants to be ready to leave here in May or early June so we can get settled over there before winter sets in. We will need to start finding a buyer for our farm soon."

"But," he added, smiling at Mother, "we will not think or talk about it anymore tonight except to place our concern before our Heavenly Father. Let us pray."

Susanna bowed her head, but before she closed her eyes, she glanced up at Father.

Father's head was not yet bowed either. It was tilted slightly back and he was looking upward. The expression on his face as he prepared to talk to God felt reassuring to Susanna.

"It will be exciting to go to America," she thought. "And whatever happens, Father and our Heavenly Father will take good care of us."

CHAPTER 3

As it turned out, not only the David Ruth and Johannes Ruth families, but all the families of the Eichstock congregation decided to go to America with Uncle Leisy.

The little church, built with such love and dedication, had served not only as a place of worship, but as a center for coming together for fellowship on other occasions. Now the building would stand empty and deserted, at least for the time being.

The Eichstock families would be joined by other families from the Palatinate, most of them from the Mannheim area. A few families were coming from the Weierhof, where the Krehbiels had lived before they came to Eichstock. They planned to leave in late May and be settled in their new homes in faraway Iowa before winter.

On February 11, 1852, Father and Uncle Johannes were able to sell their farms to Daniel Springer from Allersbach for 19,500 gulden. This sale included most of the household goods, which would remain in the houses. Since Father's buildings were worth more than Uncle John's, he received 800 gulden more of the money than Uncle John.

As soon as this sale was definite, the work of packing the things they planned to take with them began.

Father had some large crates made. Each day Mother and the older children worked at packing and repacking things so they would be able to take as much along as they needed. Getting ready to move was a fun time for the children. Each day brought something new. The excitement of the coming trip grew with each crate successfully packed.

When Grandfather Strohm heard about the plans, he decided to join the group.

"Sometimes I feel so weak and ill that I wonder whether I will still be living by the time you go," he told Mother. "But I don't want to stay here in Bavaria without you, so I'll plan to go, and hope everything works out all right."

Susanna knew that Grandfather Strohm was seventy years old. He was not well or strong. That was why he had given up his role as pastor of the Eichstock church. He was always smiling and pleasant and never complained, so it was hard to think of him as being so ill.

Mother was happy that Grandfather had decided to go with the group. But she worried that the long, exhausting journey would be too much for him.

"We must leave it all in God's hands, both Grandfather's well-being and ours," she often said. But that did not completely take away the concern that showed in her face at times.

Twenty-six-year-old Maria Dahlem and her twenty-year-old brother Gerhard decided to travel to America as part of the David Ruth family. Their mother was Father's sister Katherine. Mother was happy about this.

"It will be good to have two more grown-ups in our family to help me look after the little ones and Grandfather," she often remarked.

Susanna agreed with her. Little Jakob, who had been three in November, and Baby Maria, who was not quite a year old, were both active little youngsters. They would need to be watched, especially on the ship. And five-year-old Heinrich could not be trusted to take good care of himself either.

In mid-April Father went with others to Gruenstadt to make final arrangements for their passage on the train and ship from Mannheim to New York. From Eichstock to Mannheim the group would have to make their own travel arrangements.

When Father came home, he brought with him the

agreement he had signed with the boat company. This company would make the arrangements for the trip. He sat down at the table to show it to Mother, and the children crowded around them.

"I've put the names of Maria and Gerhard Dahlem here with ours since they will be traveling with us," he said as they looked at the first page. "See, here are all our names."

David Ruth, 43 years old
Katharina Ruth, 37 years old
Johannes Ruth, 14 years old
Susanna Ruth, 12 years old
Barbara Ruth, 10 years old
David Ruth, 8 years old
Katharina Ruth, 6 years old
Heinrich Ruth, 5 years old
Jakob Ruth, 3 years old
Maria Ruth, 1 year old
Gerhard Dahlem, 20 years old
Maria Dahlem, 26 years old

Father read on. "The first part of this contract tells us how much baggage we can take along—two hundred pounds for each adult and one hundred pounds for each child—and who pays the duty at the customs offices."

"We'll take a steamship to Cologne, where we'll stay until our departure by train for Paris and Havre. The steamship company guarantees delivery of our baggage in Havre. That takes care of items three through six." When they came to agreement number seven, Father said, "I asked them to cross this one out. I don't think we want to pay extra money to insure our baggage against shipwreck."

Mother nodded. "We will trust in God for our safety," she said. "And if our ship is wrecked and our possessions are lost, what good would the payment of this money to our attorney be to us?"

Father began to read number eight. It said that the Ruth family would take along their own food to eat on the ship.

Father asked if that was okay with Mother.

Mother nodded. "Oh yes," she said. "We will bring it with us. Then we will know just what we will have, and it will no doubt not cost as much either. I will write down what we will need and start planning for it at once."

"Sections nine and ten are important," Father said, glancing at it. "I must read them carefully. They tell what happens if we don't make our connections in time to sail on the boat from Havre."

"Number eleven assigns us space and beds in the steerage deck, free transport of our baggage, a place in the kitchen for cooking, and sufficient fresh water, wood, and light. Upon arrival in America, we will have free use of the hospital or almshouse. Our trip will cost us a total of seven hundred twenty florin.

"That is a lot of money!" Mother exclaimed as she looked at number twelve. "Yes," Father agreed, "it is a lot of money. But we will have enough money to pay that and still have enough left to buy land in Iowa when we get there. We will not have to pay all of that amount now," Father added as he began to read number thirteen. "We will be able to pay it in installments."

After Father read the last few agreements, he laid the papers carefully into the leather bag he would carry with him on the journey. Then he stood for a moment looking out of the window.

"I think I will go for a walk in the fields," he told Mother. At the door he paused and turned around.

"Now that the papers are all signed, the whole matter is so final," he said. "I still feel that going to America is God's will for us. But that does not make the leave taking from this place that has been home to me for so many years any easier."

Mother went to him and placed her hand on his arm.

"I feel what you feel," she said. "But we will all be together, and we will make a new home for our family over there."

"The whole matter is so final," Susanna thought with a shiver of happy excitement. Up until now it had all still seemed too good to be true—like a happy daydream.

"We're really going to America!" she said gleefully. "We're really going over the waters to the wonderland!"

"Over the waters to the wonderland!" Barbara and Johannes echoed. Katharina and Heinrich, and even little Jakob joined them as they chanted in chorus, "Over the waters, over the waters, over the waters to the wonderland!"

Mother walked over to join the group. "Yes," she said. "Over the waters. God is leading us over the waters."

CHAPTER 4

Finally all of the boxes were packed and nailed shut, and there were a few days left to visit with the relatives at the Schweig. Then the calendar said May 28, 1852, and it was time to leave for America! Everybody had to get up early that morning, even the little boys. Only Baby Maria could keep on sleeping in a large basket in which Mother had made a bed for her.

The heavy crates and chests in which the belongings were being transferred had been nailed shut the night before and were standing ready by the door. Bags and boxes of food and clothing that they would carry with them were piled nearby.

Breakfast was a hurried snacking of food Mother had set out the evening before, but even before they had finished eating, wagons drawn by horses or oxen began to congregate in front of the homes of the Eichstock families who were making the journey to America.

The travel company's responsibilities began at Mannheim. So Father and the others who were going from Eichstock had made their own plans to get from their homes to that place. From Augsburg to Brucksal they planned to travel by train, and from Brucksal to Heidelberg by stage coach, then on to Mannheim by train again.

But they were relying on the good will of their neighbors for the transportation from Eichstock to Augsburg, about ten miles away.

19

With the coming of the wagons, everybody had to get busy. Only Grandfather Strohm, looking forlorn and weak, remained sitting on a chair near the door beside Baby Maria's basket.

Father and the big boys started carrying out crates and boxes. Mother went with them to supervise the loading. Heinrich followed them outside. Susanna was about to pick up some bags of food and go outside, too, when she noticed little Jakob wandering around the rooms, clutching his blanket, a frightened look on his face. When he saw Susanna looking at him, he began to cry and ran to her.

"Wagons come. Men take our things," he whimpered.

Susanna picked him up and gave him a hug.

"Yes, the wagons are here," she said reassuringly. "And they're loading our things. They're going to take them to Mannheim to the railroad station for us. We'll go in one of the wagons, too. Then we'll get on the train at Mannheim. That'll be fun, won't it—riding on the train?"

Jakob looked at her with big questioning eyes.

"You don't know what I'm talking about, do you?" Susanna chuckled. "And neither do I, really. I've never even seen a train myself. But it'll be fun. You just wait and see. It'll be lots of fun."

She gave the little boy another hug and then put him down.

"Susanna has to get busy now," she told him. "You stay here and help Grandfather watch Baby Maria. Be careful that she doesn't wake up."

"Poor little tyke," she thought as she picked up some of the bags filled with food and hurried outside. "He's still half asleep, and he can't understand what's going on, even though Mother and Father and the rest of us have told and told him about going to America."

Before the sun had risen very far in the eastern sky, all of the baggage had been loaded onto the wagons and it was time for everyone to find a place to sit so that the trek could begin.

Susanna saw tears in Mother's eyes as she took a last

look around the rooms to be sure that nothing they wanted to take along had been left behind.

"I was happy here," Mother said softly to Father. "We had a good life here together."

Father's voice had a catch in it as he answered, "Yes, it has been a good life. But we must not look back. We have felt God's leading in this move, and with his help we will have a good life in the new land, too."

As she walked from the house to the wagon in which the Ruths were to ride, with little Jakob trotting beside her, Susanna felt it, too, the pain of leaving a home where she had been happy, the only home she had ever known. Each day of the past few months had been filled with excitement and anticipation at the thought of going to America, but now, suddenly, she felt that she did not really want to leave Eichstock.

Once they were in the wagon and the horses started to pull them away from Eichstock, the challenge of the new adventure won out over any sadness at what was being left behind. "We are really on the way," she said gleefully to little Jakob, who was sitting close beside her. "We are really going over the waters to America!"

It was a beautiful morning to be traveling slowly in the wagons. The fruit trees that lined the road were in full bloom. The fields were green with the young wheat just beginning to grow, and the meadows were dotted with wild flowers of many colors.

A lark, startled by the noise of the wagons, flew straight up into the air, so high that it could no longer be easily seen. Then, at that incredible height, it burst into song. The children sat entranced, listening until the song ended and the bird glided down again to feed in the meadow some distance away.

Then Mother began a song, too.

"*So nimm denn meine Hände,*" she sang softly. "Take thou my hand, O Father, and lead thou me."

It was a familiar song that the family sang often, and Father and the rest of the family joined in as they always did at home when Mother started to sing.

It was Father who started the next song, "Holy God, We

Praise Thy Name," and the group in the wagon in front of them and those in the wagon behind joined in the singing.

"Like a moving church service," Susanna thought, and then felt sad again as she thought about the little church building standing empty the next Sunday without anyone coming to worship there.

At the first crossroad, the Krehbiel family from Erlach was waiting in two wagons to join the group.

"We are a goodly number," Father remarked, looking back at the wagons following them.

"A goodly number," Johannes echoed. "How many are we?"

Johannes always liked to know exactly what was going on. So now he began to count.

"There are thirteen of us, counting the Dahlem cousins and Grandfather Strohm," he said. "Then there are Uncle John and Aunt Elsie and the six cousins. That makes twenty-one."

"Young Jakob Vogt," Father added, "and the widow Haury and her two sons, Daniel and John. That makes twenty-five. Then there are six of the Krehbiels who just joined us. So we are thirty-one persons from here."

"But at Mannheim more will join us," Mother told Johannes, "and later a few others at Worms."

At Augsburg the wagons drove to the railroad station at the edge of the town to unload the chests and other baggage at the platform near the tracks, and to let the people off near the station.

Father got out of the wagon first and took little Maria so that Mother could climb out.

"My, it feels good to stretch my legs," Mother said as she stepped down onto the ground.

Then she laughed. "I don't know when I've had time for many years to sit still as long as I did this morning," she told Father.

Her laughter changed to an expression of concern as she turned to Grandfather!

"You look so tired," she told him. "I wish you could lie down for awhile."

"I'll be all right," Grandfather assured her as Father helped him out of the wagon, but his voice was so soft that Susanna could tell that he was not feeling well.

"There should be room in the station for Grandfather to sit down," Father told Mother. "Why don't you take him in there."

As Mother and Grandfather walked slowly to the station, Father turned to Susanna and Barbara.

"You girls stay here with Maria and help watch Jakob and Heinrich. Keep an eye on the things we'll take with us into the passenger car. And if you hear the train coming before I have come back here after unloading the things that will go into the baggage car, be sure to run and help Mother with Grandfather."

Then he and Gerhard, followed by Johannes and David, hurried over to unload the crates that would go into the baggage car of the train.

By now the other members of the Eichstock group had climbed out of the wagons, and the men were busy unloading their things while the women and children began to gather by the closed gate near the train tracks. As Susanna followed cousin Maria to join them, she found herself almost trembling with excitement!

"Soon we'll get onto the train," she thought. "What will it look like? How will it feel to ride in one of the train cars?"

She knew there was no use in asking any of the others of the group these questions. None of them would know. Trains were still something very rare in Germany, and there were only a few places where one could travel on them. So none of the children and only a few of the grown-ups had even seen one, and none of the group had had a chance to ride in one.

Before long Father and most of the other Eichstock men came to join the group. A few of the young men were staying with the baggage to make sure that all of it would be loaded onto the train.

Father hurried to the station to bring Mother and Grandfather, but even before they were near the gate, a loud shrill whistle and a clickety, clackety noise on the rails announced that the train was coming. A few of the younger children began to cry and cling to their mothers and even some of the grown-ups had anxious expressions on their faces as the noisy machine came puffing toward them.

The engine was a huge black monster with many wheels which rolled along on the rails. At the front of the engine was a sort of large black shield and on the top a huge smokestack sent out puffs of black smoke. A big bell was ringing with a harsh, noisy clang that almost hurt Susanna's ears.

Behind the engine there were several coaches that looked a little like stagecoaches, except that they had more and smaller wheels.

Each coach had six doors that opened onto a narrow wooden platform running the full length of the coach. Steep ladder-like steps led down from the platform at each of the doors.

The top part of each door was glass and there were windows between the doors so that one could see the people sitting in the compartments.

When the train stopped, the doors began to open and the people walked down the steps and came toward the station, some of them carrying suitcases and bags.

An officer in a blue uniform stood very erect at the gate leading to the tracks. When the people coming from the train reached the gate, he opened it for them, and when all of them had gone through, he motioned for those who were waiting to get onto the train to come.

By now Father and Mother and Grandfather had joined the group.

Father showed their tickets to the officer, who looked at them, then motioned for the family to go through the gate. Father led the way to one of the vacant compartments toward the back of the train.

Johannes hurried up the steps to open the door and Father helped Grandfather walk up. Then he hurried down the steps again and held little Maria so that Mother could climb up. When she was at the top he handed the baby to her, then he stepped back and waited until all of the others were inside before he too climbed up and closed the door behind him.

It was a tight fit, all of them riding in the same compartment, but they wanted it that way. Nobody, not even the Dahlem cousins, wanted to be separated from the rest of the family by riding in another compartment.

They were barely settled when the bell on the engine began to clamor again and the train started to move.

The Ruth children looked at each other and began to laugh with delight as the train picked up speed and went faster and faster. Father and Mother and the cousins joined in, and even Grandfather smiled to show that he was also enjoying the ride.

The train car swayed a little, with the wheels bumping up and down at the places where the rails were fastened together, but the ride was so much smoother than the wagon had been or even than a carriage or buggy. And it went faster than Susanna would have thought anything could travel!

Soon the bell began to ring again as the train whizzed past the edge of a little village. Long bars were down along the tracks and a group of villagers, some of them in a wagon and others on foot, were waiting for the train to pass. The Ruth children waved at them through the window and the people smiled and waved back.

The train stopped at Ulm and some people got off and others got on, then big puffs of smoke floated past the window as the engine started to move the train again.

After a while Mother asked Barbara to get out the bread, cheese and apples for the noon meal. When they had finished eating, Mother said, "Now we must all take an afternoon nap. We got up early this morning, and we will be traveling all night."

Susanna did not want to go to sleep. It was too much fun to look out the window and see so many places she had never seen before. But the train swayed gently, and everything was very quiet in the compartment. She had trouble keeping her eyes from falling shut, and when she opened them again to see why Baby Maria was crying, she noticed that the trees they were passing already had long shadows, and Mother was handing out bread and cheese for the evening meal.

Before long the sun went down and it began to get dark. The forests they passed had deep, dark shadows, and here and there one could see lights from some village or town.

Susanna found herself thinking about their home in Eichstock again. Somebody else's light would be shining there from now on.

CHAPTER 5

Susanna had thoroughly enjoyed the train ride, but when the train stopped at Brucksal, she was more than ready to get off and stretch her legs.

It was dark now, but several lanterns hanging on some high poles made it possible to see the train station and a few buildings of the town. A train official, carrying a lantern, walked along the tracks, calling at the top of his voice, "Brucksal, Brucksal, everybody getting off at Brucksal, get off the train at once!"

Inside the compartment where the Ruth family was riding there was a frantic scramble to wake up all the sleepers and make sure that each piece of baggage they had with them was being carried by someone.

Finally the last of the group climbed down the stairs and everybody was ready to go on. Father, carrying sleeping Baby Maria, led the others toward the gate by the train station, and then to the nearby inn, which was also the station from which the stagecoaches would depart.

At the inn there was time for a quick snack for everyone before the vehicles in which they would be riding pulled up in front of the door and let off their passengers.

After that there was another delay while the drivers refreshed themselves before starting out on another journey, and helpers led the horses to a stable, bringing rested ones to take their place.

But finally the call came, "The coaches are ready to leave," and the Eichstock group and a few other passengers flocked outside to get on.

Several coaches pulled by four horses, two in front of the other two, and a smaller carriage pulled by two horses, were waiting in front of the inn, ready for the passengers. Father, carrying Baby Maria, led the way to one of the coaches, and the rest of the family followed.

As Susanna looked around just before she stepped into the coach, she noticed that Johannes and Gerhard were waiting with the other single men who had stepped back to let the families with children get on first.

The postilion had already mounted his horse, and the coachman was ready to close the door when it was finally Johannes's turn to get on.

As Johannes started to step into the coach where the rest of the Ruth family was riding, the coachman stopped him.

"The coach is full," he said crossly. "You can't get on here! Can't you see that there is no more room?"

"But I have to get on!" Johannes protested. "The rest of my family is in this coach. They will make room for me. I have to go with them!"

"There is no more room!" the coachman repeated angrily. Then he added, "There is plenty of room in that two-horse carriage over there. Go ride in it. It is going in the same direction we are."

When Johannes repeated, "But I have to go with the rest of my family," the coachman simply banged the door shut and walked to the front of the coach to climb up to the driver's seat.

Father, who was sitting by the window, saw that the carriage was almost ready to leave.

"Hurry!" he told Johannes, "Get into the carriage or you will be left standing here! If the carriage is going to Heidelberg also, we'll get together again there."

As the coach began to move, Susanna, looking out of the back window, saw Johannes step up into the carriage and sit down in the back seat. There were only two other passengers, an elderly couple who were riding in the front seat. "Poor Johannes!" she thought. "This will be a miserable night for him!"

It was a miserable night for the rest of the family, too! The driver of their coach was obviously drunk, and drove very recklessly. Susanna tried to go to sleep as she had done earlier on the train, but each time she began to doze off, something happened to jar her wide awake again.

A number of times the driver turned a corner so sharply that he almost upset the coach. At one place, when they were driving over a large stream, Father, who was looking out of the window, gave a little cry.

"We were in great danger just then!" he told Mother in a husky whisper. "The carriage almost went off the bridge!"

In the early morning the coaches stopped briefly at a small station to change horses, and Father stepped off the coach and looked back to see whether the carriage was coming.

"I told Johannes to get into the carriage because there seemed nothing else for him to do since the coachman wouldn't let him get in with us, and the coaches were all loaded," he said. "But I feel uneasy about Johannes not being with us. I'll stay out of the coach long enough so that I can see Johannes and he can see me. "Oh, there!" he added, "I can see it in the distance."

But almost immediately the postilion mounted his horse and the driver called out, "Everybody back into the coach! We are ready to go on."

"Well, at least we know they are not far behind us," Father said as he hurriedly climbed back into the coach. "But I would feel better if I had been able to talk to Johannes or at least to see him."

"We will trust him to God's care," Mother said reassuringly, and Father nodded.

"Johannes is in God's care. In God's care!" The words repeated themselves in Susanna's mind and presently she felt herself getting relaxed and drowsy.

When she woke up she noticed the coach was stopping at a station. It was the coachman's voice that had awakened her.

"This is Heidelberg," he was yelling. "Everybody out of the coach. We will change horses here and you will have time to eat breakfast before a different driver takes you further."

As Susanna stepped out of the coach, Father said, "Why don't you and Maria stay outside for awhile and watch for the carriage so you can tell Johannes where we are. "I'll come out again as soon as I help Mother get the little ones settled."

To Susanna's relief she soon saw a small carriage coming towards the inn, but even before it stopped she noticed that there were only two elderly passengers! Johannes was not in the carriage.

By the time the carriage stopped, Father had come outside again.

"This is a different carriage from the one that Johannes was riding in," he said, "and a different driver. We'll have to wait a little longer."

"But the other passengers are the same ones," Susanna started to say just as Father exclaimed, "But the man and the woman in the carriage are the ones with whom he was riding!"

Even before the carriage had come to a complete stop, Father was asking the couple, "What happened to the young man who got into the carriage with you at Brucksal?"

The man shrugged his shoulders.

"He didn't get on with us when we changed carriages at the last station," he said. "We don't know what he did or where he is."

The driver was upset and apologetic.

"I had no idea that I was to have more than just the two passengers," he explained. "These people got into my carriage when I was ready to go, and I didn't see anyone else."

"I remember that a young man got into the back seat of the carriage at Brucksal," the woman said. "But I don't know what he did at the station where we changed carriages. We just hurried over to this carriage when we saw that it was ready to go.

Susanna had never seen Mother as upset as she was when Father told her what the couple had said.

"What ever could have happened to him!" she wailed. "Poor Johannes! Where can he be, and what will we do?"

"There's only one thing I can think to do," Father said quietly. "I'm going to hire a buggy and go back to see whether I can find him."

"And what shall the rest of us do?" Mother asked, her voice calm now, but her face still showing her concern. "Shall we wait for you or go on to the train station with the others?"

Father thought for a moment.

"The best thing for you to do would probably be to go on with the rest of our group," he said slowly. "When I find Johannes, I'll have the driver of the buggy take us directly to the station. If the train has already gone when I get there, I'll take the next train to Mannheim."

It felt strange and a little frightening to ride in the coach without Father. Even Baby Maria and little Jakob seemed to miss him. Maria cried much of the time, and Jakob was restless and naughty. Susanna was glad when they reached the train station and could get out of the coach.

But after they were settled in seats in the train station, Susanna felt more uneasy than ever.

"I wish Father. . . " she started to say to Mother, and then she stopped. For there, coming through the door of the train station was Father, and walking behind him as though he could hardly make one foot move after the other, was Johannes!

"How did you find him so fast?" Mother gasped when the two reached her side.

Father laughed. "I didn't find him, he found us," he said. "I went to the livery stable and made arrangements to hire a buggy. While I was waiting for it just outside the door, I looked in the direction from which we had come and saw a boy walking toward the station. There was something very familiar about the way he walked, and when he came a little closer I realized it was Johannes. He recognized me at the same time and yelled 'Father!' just as I called his name."

Susanna saw tears in Father's eyes as he went on, "As we were driving over here he told me what had happened to

31

him. He had a terrible night, and I thank God that he is with us!"

Mother put her arms around Johannes. "I want to hear all about it, too," she said. Then, as a shrill whistle sounded outside, she added, "after we're all settled on the train."

Chapter 6

As soon as all of the family was seated in their train compartment, Mother turned to Johannes.

"Now tell us all about it," she said eagerly, then she chuckled as she noticed that Johannes's head was resting on the back of the seat and his eyes were closed.

"It looks as though he didn't get much sleep last night," she added.

They were almost at Mannheim when Johannes woke up and looked around him.

"I'm here with all the rest of you," he said happily. "I had an awful dream that I had been left behind, and had to walk instead of riding with you in the stagecoach."

Then as he straightened up and put his feet on the floor, he winced and shook his head.

"But it wasn't a dream, was it?" he added. "I did have to walk a long way, didn't I?"

"Yes, you must have been left behind somewhere," Mother assured him. "And you did have to walk to catch up with us. The other passengers who were in the carriage at the station at Brucksal came to the station near Heidelberg in a different carriage, but you weren't in it. What happened? You've told Father. Now the rest of us want to hear it, too."

"I was really upset when the coachman wouldn't let me squeeze in with you in the coach," Johannes said. "I didn't want to ride in that carriage. The other two passengers went to sleep soon after we left Brucksal, but I decided I wouldn't go to sleep. As long as I could see your coach ahead of us I felt all right. It was hard to keep my eyes open, but I thought I was staying awake.

"Then all at once I felt a jolt and a loud voice near the carriage yelling, "giddyap." When I opened my eyes, I noticed that our carriage wasn't moving anymore. A stable boy had unhitched the horses and was leading them away, talking loudly to them as he went. Our driver and the elderly couple weren't in the carriage anymore.

"When I looked around I saw that a short distance ahead the elderly man was helping his wife into another carriage. A different driver was climbing into the driver's seat. They had changed carriages, and nobody had awakened me so that I could change, too.

"I jumped out of the carriage I was in as fast as I could and ran toward the other carriage, which had already started to move, and I yelled as loudly as I could, 'Wait, wait, wait for me! I need to ride along, too.'

"But the carriage kept on moving, and disappeared into the darkness."

"You poor boy!" Mother said, shaking her head and patting Johannes on the shoulder. "What did you do then?"

"I didn't know what to do!" Johannes answered. "When I looked around me, I saw that we had stopped at a station on the edge of a small town, but I had no idea what the name of the place was nor how far it was from Heidelberg. The clock over the door of the station said 3 o'clock. So I must have slept about three hours.

"As I hurried to the station I was really angry at the driver. I kept thinking, Why didn't they awaken me and tell me that I should change to the other carriage? The driver knew that I was going to Heidelberg.

"When I walked into the waiting room the stationmaster and another man who were sitting at a table really looked surprised.

"The stationmaster asked me, 'Well, boy, where did you come from this time of the morning, and what do you want?'

When I told him what had happened, he shook his head in sympathy. 'There won't be any more coaches going in that direction until tomorrow evening,' he told me. 'So if you want to get there in time to catch up with your family, you'll have to walk. Or, actually, you'll have to run!'

"As I started toward the door he called to me, 'Keep on going west when you get to the fork in the road.'

"As soon as I got outside I took off my shoes and slung them over my shoulder. Then I walked as fast as I could until I got to the edge of town. Then I started to run. The words, 'If you want to get there in time,' kept whirling around in my mind. What if I didn't get there in time? What if I didn't catch up with you before you got onto the ship to go to America?

"The road was completely deserted. The moon, which was shining so brightly when we left Brucksal, was no longer in the sky, so everything was dark around me. The whole countryside was sleeping, everything was still. I had never felt so alone and frightened in my whole life.

"After awhile I came to the place where the road divided, with one branch going to the right, and the other curving slightly to the left. The stationmaster had said, 'Keep on going west.' So I took the left branch, hoping that it was going west because it curved only a little bit.

"But I wasn't sure, so I kept worrying, What if I took the wrong road? I kept on running as long as I could, then I rested by walking a little ways, and the longer I walked the more I was afraid that I'd never find you. After a while the road passed close enough to a village so that my footsteps aroused the watchdogs and they began to bark. Then I found myself worrying, What if they aren't penned up?

"I walked through several small villages and each time I was afraid that I might go out of them on the wrong road. After a while the darkness turned to dawn, and in a little while the sun came up. By that time I had to change to a walk quite often because my legs simply wouldn't run any longer.

"Finally I saw the next stagecoach station in the distance and I knew that I had almost reached the place I wanted to find. But then I felt almost sick again because I saw that there were no stagecoaches standing in front of the station. When I looked at the sun I knew that it was later than seven o'clock in the morning, and I knew that I hadn't gotten there in time.

"As I walked slowly up the street because I simply couldn't run or even walk fast anymore I saw a buggy drive up to the door of the station. A man came out of the door and looked around him before stepping into the buggy. And even at that distance I knew right away that it was Father. And I was afraid that he would drive away too before I could get to the station.

"I yelled 'Father!' and about the same time Father saw me and yelled 'Johannes' and started running toward me."

"Then we both hurried back to the buggy and drove to the train station. And fortunately we got here before the train arrived," Father said, then added, "Now let us bow our heads and thank God that we are all together again!"

CHAPTER 7

Susanna's mother and father had both grown up near Mannheim. She had heard them talk so often about friends and relatives there that she almost felt as though she knew them. So it was interesting to put faces to the familiar names during the week the travel group spent there.

It was a happy time for everybody as they visited in the different homes and got together in the church. Then it was a sad time when they had to say good-bye and go on with their travel.

"Our group will swell from thirty-one persons to fifty-seven now," Father told the family the evening before they were to leave. "Twenty-six more people will join us."

Then he named them for Mother: "Jakob Krehbiel III, his wife, mother, and six brothers and sisters; eight persons in the Schnebele family; Uncle and Aunt Leisy, and Uncle's sister Katherine; a number of single young men—Christian Springer, Johannes Frueh, Michael Wuertz, Hertzler, Knauf, and Feldman."

Uncle Leisy was now the leader of the travel group. He had crossed the ocean several times before, so for him the voyage was nothing new. The others were happy to have him for their travel leader.

From Mannheim the group went by steamboat down the Rhine to Cologne. Susanna found this part of the trip even more exciting than the train rides! There was so much to see, and they did not have to sit still, crowded into a small compartment as they had on the train. They could stand out on the deck and watch where they were going.

It was fun to stand by the railing and see the countryside go by as the boat glided down the river. On each side of the river the vineyards were green with row upon row of grapevines. Some of the men working in the vineyards waved at the boat as it went by. The passengers waved back at them.

At Worms the group got off the boat and stayed for several days. They visited friends while they waited for the Johannes Lehman family and young Philip Lehman from the Weierhof to join them. Mother was especially happy for this time for Grandfather's sake.

"He has been so weak and tired," Susanna heard Mother tell Father, "that I have really wondered whether he could go on. He himself was afraid that he should stay here in Germany after all. But today, after a day and night of rest, he feels confident that he can go with us."

Father took the older children sightseeing. Susanna especially enjoyed seeing the large cathedral with its four erect towers and two domes, and the synagogue not far from it. A little further away stood a bronze statue of Martin Luther with smaller statues around it.

After the Lehmans joined them, all seventy-two of the people traveling to America were together. The next day they started down the Rhine again, stopping briefly at Mainz, then traveling toward Cologne.

Soon after they left Mainz the banks on both sides of the river became steep hillsides. But the one on the east was still covered with vineyards.

"It's all so very different from the land around Eichstock," Johannes commented, shaking his head. "I would think the people would fall off when they're cutting their grapes on such a steep hillside!"

The hillsides on the west side of the river had no vineyards. Instead, there were rocky crags and forests with tall trees.

"Look!" David called out suddenly, "See that big building high up there on the hill!"

"That's a castle," Father explained. "We'll see many of them up in the rocky cliffs along this part of the Rhine. During the Middle Ages, lords and barons lived in these castles. It was easier for them to protect themselves and their vassals up there on the hills. And they also made every boat or barge that came past their property on the river pay a toll. So it was also a good place for them to become wealthy."

Presently the vineyards ended. There were only high rocky cliffs on both sides ahead. The water in the river flowed much faster now. Along the sides there were rapids where the water churned around and over rocks sticking out from the bottom.

Father called the children's attention to a huge boulder looming up on the east side a short distance ahead.

"That's the Lorelei," he said. He told them the legend about the mermaid who sunned herself on the rocks at the foot of the boulder. She enticed the sailors with her songs so that they forgot to steer their boats and crashed on the rocks in the rapids. They called her Lorelei.

As the boat continued on down the river, the cliffs gradually became smaller and smaller until the banks were level grassy plains again. Ahead the travelers could see the city of Cologne. Here the group planned to stop for a day.

Susanna had enjoyed the ride on the boat and all of the beautiful scenery. But it was nice to stop for a night of sleeping in an inn and a day of sightseeing in the interesting city. She had never seen anything like the huge cathedral. Father told them it had been begun 400 years ago, but was not yet finished.

The next day the group traveled by railroad train to Paris, where they again stopped for a day of sightseeing. This was long enough to cause some anxious moments for some of the parents.

Susanna was happy to stay with Mother and help her look after the little ones, but Barbara decided to go with cousin Maria to explore the city. When they did not come back by late afternoon, Mother became worried and Father asked a policeman to help look for them.

Barbara, who was not easily upset about anything, was almost in tears when Father brought them back to where the group was staying. Maria was apologetic.

"I thought we were so careful to keep track of just where we were going, but when we started to come back, we couldn't find our way," she explained.

John Lehman, who was to look after his younger brother, found so much to look at that he forgot to go back to the travel group in time and had to be looked for, too.

But everything ended well. The next morning the whole group left for Havre, where the ship on which they would go to America would be waiting for them in the harbor.

CHAPTER 8

The ship was indeed waiting in the harbor when the group arrived at Havre. Susanna got a glimpse of it from a distance as the travel group walked to the inn where they would stay until it was time for them to sail.

"We will not sail for several more days," Father told the family. "But there is much to be done before that time."

Father and the other men had to report at the office of Chrystie, Heinrich, & Company to give them a list of the baggage they were taking with them. Then they would get the papers that would allow their families to get onto the ship.

Mother and the other women took advantage of the free time to wash some clothes and do some repacking of the hand luggage. The children enjoyed playing in the sunshine in the courtyard of the inn after the days spent on trains and the riverboat.

About midmorning Father came hurrying back from the ship.

"One of our large chests burst open when it hit the bottom as it was being lowered to the storage area," he told Mother excitedly. "Some men have consented to help me try to nail it together again. The contents of the chest are all scattered. I will need your help in getting everything back into the chest again."

Mother did not get upset easily. Susanna had never seen her quite so agitated before.

"Oh my, oh my!" she wailed, throwing up her hands. "We spent weeks getting as much as possible packed into those chests. Now I'm to do it all over again in a few hours?"

She put on her scarf and hurried to the ship with Father.

In the late afternoon the two came back to the inn with smiling faces to report that everything had gone well. The chest had been repaired, and they had managed nicely to get everything back inside.

"But I will feel relieved when we're all settled on the ship," Mother added with a sigh.

The sailing date for the Samuel Fox was May 28. Early that morning the women and children had a chance to get their first good look at the ship.

Uncle Leisy's group was traveling steerage class, which meant they were paying the lowest fare. Their accommodations would not be as comfortable as those traveling first class. They had to wait with the other steerage class passengers until all the other passengers had gone aboard before they could walk onto the ship.

This gave them plenty of time to get a good look at the vessel.

Compared to the Rhine steamer, it was huge. The Samuel Fox was a 1,500 ton, three-masted English vessel with thirty-two white sails raised majestically toward the sky.

Susanna felt a thrill of excitement when it was finally their turn to walk up the gangplank to the deck. They walked down one flight of stairs after another until they reached the large room where they would be living with the other steerage class passengers.

Except for some hand luggage they carried with them, the baggage, including the food boxes, had all been brought to the boat the day before. It was stored in large bins along two sides of the room. On a third side there were some built-in tables and benches. The rest of the space in the room was filled with beds. The beds looked like thin mattresses. They were suspended like hammocks in three tiers from rods extending from the ceiling to the floor.

None of the bunks were specifically assigned to any group or persons, so the women in the Leisy group lost no time claiming berths for their families. The young unmarried men in the group chose some bunks in a far corner of the room.

The first thing Mother did after the family had decided on their sleeping places was to put some bedding onto one of the bottom bunks so that Grandfather Strohm could lie down. Father helped Maria and the girls put away the hand luggage under the bunks. Then he and Johannes took the younger children up onto the deck while the girls helped Mother make up the other beds.

When they had finished their work downstairs, Mother and the girls also went up to the deck. It was so crowded with people that it took them some time to find Father and the younger children standing near the railing looking out over the water.

"My, what a crowd there is on the ship!" Mother said to Father, shaking her head. "I wonder how many people there are."

"I was just talking to some of the young men of our group a little while ago," Father answered. "They said the captain told them there would be about 700 passengers. The captain has asked these fellows to help him pull up and draw in the smaller sails each day."

"I'm sure they're glad about that," Mother commented. "It will give them something to do during the long weeks we'll be sailing."

"They also told me," Father went on, "that the captain had told them we will not be able to sail today. The water here in the harbor is not deep enough because of the neap tide."

"That sounds fine to me," Mother decided. "It will give us a little time to get settled in our temporary home before we get out on the ocean. One of the things I must do this afternoon is to find the kitchen where we can cook our meals."

As the sun rose higher and higher in the sky, more and more of the people began to go to their cabins or to the steerage area or the dining room.

"I think we should go downstairs, too," Father commented, and led the way down the steps.

When they were all downstairs, Mother got out a sack of zwieback and some slices of ham.

"This will have to suffice for today," she said. "This afternoon I'll find a kitchen, and tomorrow we can have something cooked to eat."

Later in the afternoon Susanna went with Mother and some of the other Eichstock women to check on the cooking facilities. They found that there were four kitchens on the ship. One was for the ship's crew, one was for the first class passengers, and two were for the steerage passengers. Each kitchen was about twelve feet long, with a stove on each side running the full length of the kitchen.

"Only four stoves for all of us crowded together in the steerage part of the ship!" Aunt Leisy exclaimed. "How will we manage to all get our cooking done every day?"

"We'll have to get up early," one of the women answered. Another one laughed and said, "Or do our cooking late, after the others are done."

"I'll plan things so I won't have to cook every day," Mother decided. The other women agreed with that.

Bedtime came early for the steerage passengers since lighted candles or lamps were not allowed in the hold.

Mother and some of the other women had pinned up sheets to curtain off the sleeping areas for their families so they would have some privacy. But there was still friendly chatter across the room as Uncle Leisy's group prepared for bed, with giggles and laughing shrieks as the children who were sleeping on upper bunks used the rope ladders for the first time to climb to their beds. It was all like a merry party.

When all of his family was settled for the night, Father began to softly sing their bedtime song. Many of the others in Uncle Leisy's group joined in:

Muede bin ich, geh zu Ruh,	Tired am I and seek repose,
Schliesse mein Augen zu;	As my weary eyelids close,
Vater, lass die Augen dein	Father, let your eyes of love
Ueber meinem Bette sein.	Keep watch o'er me from above.

44

After the song ended, the room became quiet. Soon Susanna felt herself dropping off to sleep. Drowsily she thought, "We're far away from Eichstock now. And America seems even farther away. But Father and our Heavenly Father will take good care of us."

The next morning when Susanna went with Mother to one of the steerage kitchens, they found all of the stove area was already full. In the second kitchen only one of the stoves was full. The second one was still empty, but there was no fire in it. So Mother had to build a fire before she could set her pot on to cook the food.

By the time the fire was burning well enough for the water in Mother's kettle of potatoes to boil, enough more women had come that all the spaces on the second stove were filled.

Before Mother's potatoes were done, a woman whom Susanna did not know, came to the door of the kitchen with a kettle full of food to cook. Seeing that all of the places on the stove were taken, she scowled angrily.

"How am I supposed to get my meal cooked if there is no room on the stove?" she shouted. "My husband and children are hungry!"

Mother's kettle was on the cooking space nearest to the door. Susanna gasped as the woman grabbed it and threw it out into the hall, then set her own kettle on the space where it had been.

The other women in the room stared angrily, and for a moment Mother was nonplussed. Then she turned and walked out into the hall to retrieve her kettle, which fortunately had landed with the bottom on the floor. Nothing except a little water had spilled out of it.

Picking up the kettle, Mother turned and walked back into the room to stand beside the woman.

"I'm sorry," she said quietly. "You should have told me that you were in such a hurry. I would have taken my kettle off myself to let you have the space."

The woman glared at Mother without answering, and then her face got red with embarrassment. Without saying anything more, Mother took her kettle to the other stove, where a space had become vacant.

In the evening a few days later, the ship was finally towed by a steamboat out into the ocean. The deck was crowded as all of the passengers wanted to watch it begin to sail.

"And to say good-bye to our homeland," Mother said wistfully, a catch in her voice.

Father had managed to get a place near the railing of the boat for the family, so they had a good view after they got out into the open ocean. It was thrilling to watch the sails flare out as the wind pushed them, and to look toward the sunset in the west. As far as the eye could see, there was nothing ahead of them except water and more water meeting the horizon in the distance.

We're really on our way over the waters to the wonderland, Susanna thought, shivering a little with excitement. How huge the waters looked! And how very far away America must be!

The first days of the voyage were like a delightful vacation. The weather was sunny and the sea was calm. The men sat on the deck and visited. Some of the women had brought along knitting or other handwork. Others supervised their children's play. Some strolled together along the railing watching the waves, or sat together on the deck visiting with friends and making new ones.

Then suddenly everything changed!

Stormy weather set in, making it almost impossible to go out onto the deck because of the fury of the waves and the pouring rain. Whenever a wall of waves hit the ship, it tilted over on its side so that even down in the steerage room the floor became like a steep roof. The baggage that was not fastened down was constantly thrown violently back and forth, and the passengers had difficulty keeping their balance. It was impossible to lie on the upper bunks. Even huddled together on the lower ones and holding on to each other, it was not easy to get any sleep.

Most of the passengers suffered from seasickness. The

stench of their vomit added to the discomfort of all of the passengers. Grandfather Strohm lay in a stupor, and Baby Maria cried almost constantly. She did not want to eat or drink, and her little body became thin and weak.

Finally, one morning the wind and the rain lessened. After a short time the storm stopped entirely. The sun shone again, the sea became calm, and the boat ceased its tossing.

Then another danger threatened.

Word got around early one morning that mutiny had broken out among the sailors. A group of them were threatening to set the ship on fire and flee in the lifeboats.

There was no relaxed visiting on deck that day, or leisurely strolling along the railing watching the sea. All of the passengers stayed in their quarters. The Leisy group spent the time in prayer.

Fortunately before evening there was good news. The majority of the crew had remained loyal. With their help the mutineers were overpowered and locked up in chains to be turned over to the authorities in New York.

Slowly life on board the ship came back to what it had been before the storm. Many of the seasick people began to recover in the sunshine on the deck. The sleeping quarters were cleaned and straightened up. The children began to play games again. The grown-ups sat together in groups to visit.

But not all of the sick recovered. There were twelve deaths, among them Uncle Leisy's twenty-nine-year-old sister, Katherine, who died of typhoid fever. Like the others, she was lowered to her grave in the deep ocean while her friends and family mourned.

For Father and Mother her illness and death brought a new worry. Katherine had lain in their bed while she was ill. Would they or one of the children become sick with the dreaded disease? They prayed earnestly that God would spare them, and thanked him daily when none of the rest of the family became ill.

The storm had blown the ship far north off course. One day a passenger discovered a new diversion to the boredom of the voyage. Some whales were sighted nearby! After that, standing on deck and looking for more whales became a favorite pastime for everybody.

The day in July when they were to have arrived at New York came and went without any sight of land. This meant another serious problem faced those aboard the ship.

Food supplies and even drinking water became scarce. The passengers had to bathe and wash their clothes in seawater. Mother began carefully to ration what was left of the zwieback and potatoes.

Finally, on the afternoon of the third of August, the cry came, "Land! Land! See over there, I see land!"

Even Grandfather let Father help him up the steps to look. That evening Mother could be generous with the zwieback left in the sack.

To the children's great disappointment they had to go to bed and sleep before the ship came close enough for them to really see the wonderland. But the next morning it was there, just ahead of them. After a good look at it, they gleefully hurried down to steerage to help Mother pack up the baggage they would carry with them when they went on shore.

CHAPTER 9

The first days in America were not at all what Susanna had expected, and she found herself homesick for Eichstock.

The responsibility of the Gentlemen Chrystie, Heinrich, and Company ended as soon as the passengers stepped off the boat and their baggage had all been unloaded.

No specific arrangements had been made beforehand for their stay in New York City until they could travel on. So the group had to wait on the pier, surrounded by their belongings until Uncle Leisy and some of the other men checked on a place for them to stay while they were in the city.

There was no shelter or shade on the pier, and the summer sun beat down on the group while they waited. Father made a seat by putting some bedding onto one of the chests so that Grandfather and Mother, who was holding Baby Maria, could sit down. But there was nothing to shade them from the hot sun.

Poor Grandfather looked so weak and tired, as though he might faint at any time, and Baby Maria lay listlessly on Mother's lap, whimpering fretfully now and then.

After what seemed hours, Uncle Leisy and the men who had gone with him came back to report that arrangements had been made for the hold baggage to be taken to the railroad station where it would be stored until the group was ready to put it onto a train. And the combination hotel-boarding house on the quay had room for all of the Leisy group for as long a time as they needed to stay in New York.

Some of the younger children hopped and skipped as the group walked over to the hotel, and Susanna felt like joining them. After the weeks of being cooped up on the ship, it felt so good to be walking on land again!

On Sunday morning a woman from the American Tract Society came to the hotel to offer to take the group to a church where services were held in the German language.

"How thoughtful of her," Mother exclaimed as she hurried to get her family ready to go. "Even though we had our own worship services on the ship, it hasn't seemed like Sunday since we left Eichstock!"

The services were different from the ones that Susanna was accustomed to, but it felt good to be sitting in a church again, and she was happy when the group decided to go back again for the evening service. But she was frightened when soon after the group had started out, some people on the other side of the street began throwing rocks at them and yelling, "Green Germans! Green Germans!"

She had not expected people in America to act like that!

On Monday morning Susanna and Barbara helped Mother and cousin Maria repack some of the suitcases and do laundry. Then in the afternoon, with nothing more interesting to do, they joined some of the other older girls who were standing outside the hotel watching the people go by.

Most of the people paid no attention to the group of girls except to glance at them as they walked by. But presently a young woman dressed in a pretty, bright-colored dress and wearing a large, beautiful hat, stopped to talk. To the girls' surprise this finely dressed young women knew their language.

"I heard you speaking German," she said, smiling at them. "That was my native tongue, too. Did you just come over from Germany?"

"Yes," one of the girls answered, "we got off the boat the day before yesterday."

"I see you are all wearing scarves," the woman continued. "Here in America we wear hats. Now that you are going to be Americans, I think you should also each have a hat to wear. I'll tell you what. You come with me and I'll see that you each get a hat. And they won't cost you a penny. I'll see to that."

Smiling at Susanna, who was the one standing closest to her, she took hold of her hand.

"Yes, come with me," she said pleasantly. Then to the others, as she led Susanna down the sidewalk, "All of you come. You'll enjoy seeing the hats."

At first Susanna hung back and tried to pull away her hand, thinking about the rock-throwing crowd the evening before. And Mother had warned that if they went outside they must be careful of strangers walking by.

Looking back, Susanna relaxed when she saw that the other girls were also following. This woman was really not a stranger. She was a German like they were. And it would be interesting to see the pretty hats, even though she knew that Mother and Father would never allow her to wear such a worldly thing.

Even though the woman continued to talk pleasantly, asking about their trip and telling about her coming to America, Susanna began to feel more and more uneasy as they got further away from the hotel entrance. Turning around to say something to her friends, she noticed that the other girls had all turned around and were walking back to the hotel.

"Thank you for offering us the hats," she said quickly to the woman. "But I don't think I should go with you. Mother told us not to go away from the hotel, so I must go back now."

To her surprise the woman did not let go of her hand. Instead, she tightened her grip.

"You are not going back to the hotel," she said emphatically. "You are going with me!" Her voice was no longer friendly and pleasant, and her eyes looked hard and angry.

Susanna tried to pull her hand away and turn around, but the woman was stronger than she was. A feeling of fear and panic made Susanna suddenly feel sick! Who was this woman and why did she not want to let her go back to the hotel?

They had come to the end of the block, and the woman was pulling her around the corner, when a shrill whistle

51

pierced the air.

A loud voice shouted in German, "You there, stop that! Let that girl go! I know who you are, and I'll report you to the police!"

Looking back over her shoulder Susanna saw the hotel manager running after them, waving his hands and shouting again, "I'll report you to the police!"

Even before the second yell, the woman had let go of Susanna's hand and disappeared as fast as she could around the corner.

Panting from his run and still sputtering in anger, the manager walked back to the hotel with Susanna.

"You are fortunate that I happened to be by the door when the other girls got back so they could tell me what had happened. Otherwise your parents would probably never have seen you again. That varmint! She looks like a nice person, but she's an evil woman from a den of iniquity. Whatever made you go along with her?"

"I thought it would be interesting to see the pretty hats she promised to buy us, even though I knew Mother would never let me wear one," Susanna told him. "She was so friendly, and she spoke German."

"Not all people who speak German are good people," the hotel manager answered emphatically, then muttered again, "That woman!"

Mother said the same thing with tears in her eyes when she found out what had happened.

"Not all Germans are good people," she said. "And while most Americans are good people, it is better not to trust any of them that we do not know, especially here in the big cities."

Susanna had trouble going to sleep that evening. She could not get the woman, who spoke German so fluently and was so friendly and looked so elegant in her stylish dress and pretty hat, out of her mind.

She still did not quite understand what had almost happened to her. Just what did it mean, "an evil woman from a den of iniquity?" Whatever it meant, it seemed to be something evil and dangerous.

She felt betrayed by her wonderland!

Susanna was more than happy when the group went on by steamboat up the Hudson River to Albany, New York. From there they rode on a train to Buffalo, New York.

When they got off the train at Buffalo, Susanna could hardly believe that they were at a train station. It was so different from the stations in Germany! There was no building where passengers could wait. It was simply an open yard where the baggage could be put after it was unloaded from the train.

When he was making the travel plans in Germany, Uncle Leisy had suggested that the group plan to stay in Buffalo long enough so that those who wanted to could go to see the spectacular Niagara Falls. Mother and Father had planned to take the family to see the falls, and Susanna had been looking forward to it. But now it seemed that Father and Mother would have to make a choice since the group was scheduled to stay only one day and a night in Buffalo.

Mother was upset when she found out about this. "I would very much like to see the falls," she told Father, "but I've been looking forward to visiting Aunt Anna Frei, Mother's sister, who lives here in Buffalo. Now it will be hard to decide which one to do."

Before Father could answer, Mother went on, "Since we cannot do both, we will visit Aunt Anna. The falls will no doubt be there for many more years, and perhaps we can go to see them some other time after we are settled in America. But Aunt Anna is old enough so that this may be the last chance we will have to visit her."

So the next morning the whole Ruth family and Grandfather Strohm went with Uncle and Aunt Leisy to visit Aunt Anna. Susanna was unhappy about Mother's choice. She really wanted to see the falls instead of an elderly aunt. But, of course, she did not say so. And when Aunt Anna opened the door for her visitors, Susanna was glad they had come.

Aunt Anna was so happy to see them that there were tears in her eyes. And she kept saying, "It's so long since I last saw you, and I didn't expect to ever see you again!"

But Aunt Anna had bad news for them.

"Cholera is prevalent in the city," she told Uncle Leisy. "Let's hope that no one in your group gets it."

"Cholera?" Uncle Leisy almost shouted, getting up quickly from his chair. "Cholera here in Buffalo? If I had known that, we would not have planned to stop here!"

Then he sat down again.

"Well," he said, his voice quieter, but still strained. "Since we cannot leave Buffalo before the group gets back from the falls, I might as well relax and enjoy this visit. But we will not spend the night here as we had planned."

"Let's hope that none of the group was exposed while we were waiting at the train station," Father said quietly. "From what I have heard the disease is very contagious."

To Aunt Anna's disappointment, Uncle Leisy would not even stay for the afternoon coffee time before he hurried the visitors back to the train station where they were to meet those of the group who had gone to the falls.

Susanna could see that Mother was disappointed, too, that the visit with Aunt Anna was so short, especially when they had to wait at the train station while Uncle Leisy went to the pier to make arrangements for the group to leave on the next steamboat going from Buffalo to Cleveland, Ohio.

All of the time that they were waiting, Susanna found herself worrying about cholera. What would happen if one of the travel group did get sick? Would all of the rest of them get cholera, too? What if Father or Mother got sick?

She felt more worried than ever when the sightseers got back and she noticed that Mr. Lehman looked pale and held onto Mrs. Lehman as he walked. Was that how people acted when they had cholera?

While the group was walking to the wharf, Mr. Lehman began to vomit, and by the time they got to the boat, it took several men to help him onto the deck. Instead of trying to get him down the stairs, they fixed a place on the deck for him where he could lie down.

As the Ruth family walked down the steps to the

lounge, Susanna saw Mother and Father looking at each other as they did sometimes when something was worrying them. And early in the evening when Mother was getting the family settled down for the night, eight-year-old David began to cry.

"I don't feel good!" he told Mother, then before she could respond, he began to vomit.

"David, oh, David!" Mother said, her voice high pitched and strained.

As Susanna tried to find something with which to clean up the mess, she found herself shaking. Vomiting, she remembered, was one of the symptoms of cholera!

"I heard that there is a doctor on board the boat," Father said quietly. "I'll see whether I can find him. Perhaps he would have some medicine we can give David."

It seemed ages before Father came back carrying a small bottle full of a liquid.

"The doctor gave me this," he said, handing the medicine to Mother. "And he suggested that we make a bed for him in a corner of the deck cabin to keep him away from the other passengers." Father picked David up in his arms and Mother took the blanket she had laid on the bench where David was to sleep. Then they walked together up the stairs to the deck.

Susanna tried to make herself comfortable on one of the benches so that she could go to sleep. But she felt frightened. Cholera must be a terrible disease to have upset Uncle Leisy, and now Mother and Father, so much. What if little David became very sick? What if he even died?

She was still wide awake with her eyes staring at the ceiling when Mother came back down the stairs. Quickly she closed her eyes so that Mother would not notice that she had not gone to sleep. But Mother stopped at her bench.

"Are you having trouble sleeping, Susanna?" she asked softly, patting Susanna's cheek gently with her hand. "Father is staying with David. All we can do now is to pray to God to help our David get well."

Then Mother folded her hands over Susanna's as she used to do when Susanna was a small child. She did not say any words out loud, but Susanna knew that she was praying.

"O Heavenly Father," Susanna prayed silently, too, "Please, if it is your will, help our David get well."

By the time Mother was settled on the bench were Maria and little Maria were sleeping, Susanna felt herself dropping off to sleep, too.

When she awakened some time during the night, she noticed that Mother was no longer on her bench.

"She must have gone upstairs to be with Father and David," Susanna thought. "I hope that doesn't mean that David is worse!"

On impulse she slipped off her bench and walked as quietly as she could up the steps to the deck. When she got out onto the deck, she noticed that their boat had stopped at the pier of some small town. Mother and Father were standing close together just outside the deck cabin door, looking at a woman and some children who were standing at the railing.

As she slipped over to stand with Father and Mother, Susanna realized that the woman at the railing was Mother Lehman, and that she and the children were sobbing. Mother and Father did not notice Susanna until she stood beside them. Then Father reached out his arm and pulled her close to him.

"Father Lehman died!" he told her quietly. "The box the crewmen are carrying is his coffin. He will be buried in a cemetery in this little town."

"And David?" Susanna asked in a whisper, fighting back her tears, "Will David die, too?"

"David has gone to sleep," Father told her, "and we hope that is a good sign. But we do not know. All we can do is pray that our Heavenly Father will let us keep him with us. Now go back downstairs and try to go to sleep again."

As the boat began to move again, Father and Mother hurried over to Mother Lehman and her children, who had started to walk slowly away from the railing. Mother put her arm around Mrs. Lehman, and Father knelt down beside two of the smaller boys and held them close.

As Susanna walked slowly back downstairs, a frightening thought pushed itself into the back of her mind, "If God let Father Lehman die, maybe he won't help our David get well either."

She lay down on the bench, but it took a long time before she dropped off to sleep again.

When she woke up in the morning, she heard Mother happily humming a hymn as she rummaged through the food bag.

As Susanna sat up, Mother looked at her and smiled. "Our David is hungry," she said in a happy voice. "So I came down here to get something for him to eat."

There was a happy spring in Mother's steps as she hurried back up the stairs, and Susanna found herself wanting to clap her hands and shout.

By afternoon David wanted to get up and play with the other children on the deck, and by the next day he seemed to be completely well again.

CHAPTER 10

The steamboat stopped for a short time at Cleveland, Ohio, but not long enough for the travelers to get off and look at the town. Then it went on to Toledo, Ohio.

Susanna had enjoyed riding on the boat. When she remembered how much fun their first train rides in Germany and France had been, she was happy when Uncle Leisy announced, "We'll get off at Toledo and go by train to Chicago."

To her disappointment she found out that the American trains were not like those in Europe! Instead of having small compartments like the German train had, the train they got onto at Toledo had cars with no partitions. There were only wooden benches on each side of a long aisle down the middle of the car.

And instead of whizzing quickly from one town to another, the trains seemed to take forever to get the travelers to the places they wanted to go. In one town the train stopped on the main track all night. Even Uncle Leisy could not find out just what the trouble was nor when the train would go on. The passengers did not dare leave the train to find a place to sleep.

Susanna was happy when they changed trains in a small town. But the train they got onto turned out to be even more uncomfortable than the one on which they had been riding. It had only freight cars, which had no seats or benches at all.

The passengers had to either sit on the floor or on their luggage if they did not want to ride standing up.

This train took even longer than the passenger train to get to its destination. In one town it stopped on the main track from early in the morning until late in the evening. Food was getting scarce by this time because no one had expected to be on the way that long. Several of the young men offered to go into the town and forage for food.

They were not very successful. Michael Wuertz came back with some buttermilk, and Hertzler with some pancakes.

"I'm glad Mother brought along as much food for us as she did," Susanna thought. "But we've already eaten all of it. There is nothing left to share."

It was pitch dark by the time the train began to move. Susanna, lying on a blanket, crowded in between Barbara and Katharine, found it hard to go to sleep. Each time that she thought she was dozing off, a hard jolt or a loud whistle from the train engine awakened her.

It was a miserable night!

When the train finally stopped at Chicago early in the morning, Susanna said a special "thank you" prayer.

It was a sunny day. Susanna decided that the walk along a large body of water, which Uncle Leisy called Lake Michigan, on the way to their hotel was the most enjoyable thing that had happened since they got to America.

"The water is so clean we could wash our dirty clothes in it," Mother remarked. Susanna knew from the way she said it that she was jesting. But Mother's sister, Aunt Leisy, took her seriously.

"Why don't we?" she suggested. "I've been wishing I could wash some of our clothes. I think we won't find a better place to do it until we get to the end of our trip."

The afternoon turned into a sort of festival. The women and older girls had a merry time while they washed and rinsed, then spread the clothes out on the grass to dry. The young men and older boys explored the shore of the lake. The fathers sat on the bank and talked. They kept an eye on the children who played on the soft grass. Susanna was unhappy when it was time to go back to the hotel.

There were no railroads going west from Chicago, so early the next morning the trip continued on toward the Illinois River in a canal boat pulled by two horses that walked on the bank of the canal.

Next to the stormy days on the ocean, this was the most uncomfortable part of the whole trip, Susanna decided before they had gone very far.

The boat moved slowly, slowly, slowly, at a snail's pace. Water and foam from the canal splashed over the sides. The hot sun burned down on the open deck where the passengers had to sit. Time and again the boat grounded on a sandbank, and the young men had to step off the boat into the mire and help push it until it would go forward again.

This happened so often that some of the young men decided to keep on walking along on the bank instead of coming back onto the boat each time. Suddenly, without any warning, the boat turned into the Illinois River and the young men were left behind. Fortunately Father noticed what was happening, and reacted quickly.

Yelling at a man who was fishing from a boat nearby, he held up a quarter and indicated that he would give it to him if he helped the fellows. The man seemed to understand immediately what had happened, and brought the young men back to the canal boat in his rowboat.

The travel group had intended to go to St. Louis, but when they found out that there was cholera there, they got off the boat in Peoria. The widow Lehman parted from the others and traveled with her children and baggage to Fort Madison.

Baby Maria had become sick again on the overland journey, and the long ride had been almost too much for Grandfather Strohm. So Father and Mother took them both to a physician at Peoria. But the treatment he gave them did not make them feel any better.

From Peoria the travelers rode in a mail coach to Burlington, Iowa, where they stayed for the rest of the day and spent the night. Then it was time for good-byes. From here on each family was on its own. They were not all going to the same place. Susanna felt almost as sad when she said good-bye to some of her friends as she had when they left Eichstock.

About sixty people were going to West Point, Iowa: the two Ruth families, Grandfather Strohm, the Dahlems, and the "Erlacher" Krehbiel family. Uncle and Aunt Leisy were traveling with them, although they planned to go on from West Point to Summerfield, Illinois.

Father and the other men in the group hired some farmers to take the families from Burlington to West Point in their wagons. The final part of their long journey had begun.

As they rode slowly over prairie land, past fields and through small forests, Susanna found herself thinking about their ride in the wagons from Eichstock to Augsburg when they were leaving for America. At that time she had been torn between not wanting to leave their nice Eichstock home, where the family had had so many good times, and eagerness to go to the wonderland.

Now, almost three months later, she was here in America and eager to get to their new home. But she still felt homesick for the home they had left at Eichstock.

It was evening and dark enough that lights were shining in the windows of the homes in West Point by the time the travelers got there. At one house some people with lanterns were sitting in front of the house. As Father pulled on the reins to stop the horses, a man's voice called, "They're here!" The other wagons stopped, too. Before anybody had time to climb out of the wagons they were surrounded by friends who had been waiting for them.

"We're finally, finally here!" Susanna thought as she climbed out of the wagon. How good it felt to know that the long trip was over!

The families spent the night in the homes of friends. The next day Father and Uncle John each rented an empty house in West Point for their families to live in until they could find some land to buy. Then they hired wagons and teams to go back to Peoria and bring the chests of household goods that had been left there because there was no room to take them on the mail coach.

When Father got back, the whole family helped unload and unpack the boxes. Friends loaned them necessary furniture until they could buy some. By evening the rented house began to feel almost like home.

CHAPTER 11

America was different from Bavaria, and West Point was not at all like Eichstock! All of the Ruth family agreed on that. And at first Susanna was not at all sure that she liked living in the wonderland.

For one thing, even before they were really settled in their rented home, the whole family became sick with the ague, an illness that gave them a fever that gave them chills and made them shiver and ache all over their bodies. And Father's rheumatism became worse than it had ever been.

To the whole family's relief, after he had spent the first few days resting in bed, Grandfather began to feel stronger than he had for months. He not only got up from his bed, but walked around in the house and visited with friends who came to see whether there was anything they could do to help the family get settled.

Unfortunately the improvement did not last long. One morning Grandfather did not feel like getting up. When Mother noticed that his face and hands were beginning to look puffy and swollen with fluid, she sent Father to the doctor to get some medicine for Grandfather's dropsy. But the medicine did not seem to help him, and he grew weaker and weaker each day.

Baby Maria was still very sick, too. She didn't like the medicine the doctor prescribed for her, and fought taking it. She cried so much that Mother had to spend hours each day

63

looking after her.

Neighbors and friends brought in food and checked on how things were going. Some of them even stayed at times to sit at Grandfather's bedside. Even though Father was in constant pain himself, and the ague made Susanna and Barbara feel miserable, they tried to help Mother all they could. But they did not really know how to nurse Grandfather, and Baby Maria did not want anyone except Mother to take care of her. Before long the physical strain began to show on Mother's face. She looked tired all the time, and Susanna began to worry that she would become sick, too.

One afternoon when Susanna answered a knock at the door, she saw a young man dressed in a white suit standing there.

The man grinned at her and said, "Well, good day, Susanna."

Instead of asking the man to come in, Susanna stared at him. The voice sounded familiar. And the young man looked like—but it couldn't be!

The man threw back his head and laughed.

"Have I changed so much in a year and a half that you don't even know me anymore?" he asked. "I didn't think you would forget me that fast."

Susanna felt herself blushing in embarrassment.

"Christian," she stammered. "Christian Krehbiel! Of course, I remember you! But I didn't expect to see you here. I thought you were living in Ohio. Your father had written . . ."

Chuckling again, Christian asked, "May I please come in?" and answering his own question, stepped inside. "I'm sorry to have surprised you so. But I was in West Point and . . ."

Father must have heard and recognized Christian's voice also, because he came limping into the room before Christian could finish his sentence.

"I thought I heard," Father began, then he looked at Christian. "It is you! How did you get here? I thought you were living in Ohio."

"We were living in Ohio," Christian said, "but land was so expensive there that Father could not afford to buy any. So the family moved to Iowa this spring. But I had already come with some other young men in the fall. We didn't write to you about it because we knew you were already on the way. And I just heard today about Grandfather Strohm's illness. We didn't even know for sure that you were already here."

"Has your father bought land here?" Father wanted to know.

"He bought a hundred acres out on the Franklin Prairie, which cost him $800," Christian answered. "He would have liked to buy more, but after the expense of buying Jakob's freedom from the military draft in Bavaria and the passage over here for our family, he didn't have enough money."

"Is it good farm land? Are there buildings on it?" Father asked.

"Seventy acres are still in virgin forest," Christian answered. "And there were no buildings on the place. At first we lived with the Walkers, the family from whom Father bought the land. Then neighbors helped us build a one and a half story log house and a log barn from trees cut down in our own woods."

Susanna found herself thinking about the well-kept farmyard and the roomy house on the Waspelhof where the Krehbiels had lived in Bavaria.

"Will we have to live in a small log house here, too?" she wondered.

By now the rest of the family must also have heard and recognized Christian's voice because Mother came hurrying into the room, followed by Barbara and Katharine and the boys.

"Oh, Christian, Christian, I'm so happy to see you," Mother said, and began to cry.

Christian put an arm around her. "And I'm happy to see all of you and to know that you arrived safely. It seems a long time since we used to have such good times together in Bavaria."

"But we are forgetting our manners," Mother said, wiping her eyes with her apron, "letting you stand here in the doorway. Won't you come in and sit down. And please excuse

65

me. I hear Baby Maria crying, and I had not finished looking after Grandfather.

"Wait," Christian said as Mother turned to leave the room. "That's why I came. I heard about Grandfather Strohm being sick. I'm sure you noticed the white uniform I'm wearing. I had some training and experience in nursing in Ohio, and now I've been nursing one of my cousins here in West Point. However, he's much better and doesn't need me anymore. So I came to see if I could help nurse Grandfather Strohm."

Mother had to wipe away tears again.

"You don't know how good it will feel to have your help!" she said. "Just this morning I pleaded with God to give me the strength to hold out."

So Christian came over every day from his cousin's house to nurse Grandfather. Susanna found herself watching him in surprise. This seemed to be a different Christian Krehbiel from the boy she had known in Eichstock! That one had been impatient, a hard worker who wanted to get things done right and in a hurry, and who didn't hesitate to tell others what they should do also. But now, with Grandfather, Christian was as patient and gentle as the kindest woman could have been. And even Baby Maria let him carry her around in his arms.

But even Christian's skillful nursing didn't help Grandfather get better, and on September 2 he went to sleep in the afternoon and did not wake up. When Mother went in to check on him, she found that he had died.

After a memorial service in the rented home, he was buried in the Methodist cemetery at West Point since the Mennonites did not yet have a burial place. And Christian Krehbiel went back to his home on the Franklin Prairie.

For days Susanna did not feel like doing anything except cry, and the rest of the family seemed to be feeling the same way. Mother kept saying, "The long trip was just too much for him. Perhaps I should have talked him out of coming with us. He could have stayed in Bavaria with one of my brothers."

Then she would reassure herself, "But he so very much

wanted to come with us! And I think I would rather have him here where I can visit his grave than to worry about how he was getting along in faraway Bavaria!"

During most of September the weather continued to be warm and humid, but by mid-October the sun shone most of the time and the air was clear and crisp. Both the ague and Father's rheumatism seemed to notice the change because the whole family except for Baby Maria began to feel better.

While Grandfather had been so sick, and everyone else feeling so miserable, the Ruth family had not even considered going to church, and for Susanna Sundays had not seemed like Sundays at all. But now that Father was feeling better, he decided it was time for them to start going to the worship services.

The Mennonite church was about four miles from West Point, so it wasn't as easy for the family to walk together to church as it had been at Eichstock. But Father had already bought a wagon and a team of horses in preparation for starting to look for land to buy. So on Sunday morning he hitched the team to the wagon and everyone except Mother and Baby Maria climbed in. Father had decided that even little Jakob was old enough to go.

Riding to church in the new wagon was more interesting than walking the short distance to church at Eichstock had been, Susanna decided. And she was fascinated with the church building. It was made of logs and stood at the edge of a lovely evergreen forest. All of the people were friendly, and most of them had known Father and Mother in Germany. So it did not take long for Susanna to feel at home with them.

The minister, Heinrich Ellenberger, was an elderly man who had himself come from the Palatinate, Germany, only a short time before. The services were much like the ones in Eichstock, with the same hymns and the same kind of worship. When the services were over, Susanna felt almost as though she had been worshiping in the little Eichstock church again.

In the next few days Susanna felt better about being in America than she had since they had come. But she was still unhappy and concerned about one thing. Baby Maria continued to grow worse.

She cried in a feeble whimper almost constantly whenever she was awake. For several days she wouldn't eat or drink anything, and finally in the evening of December 9 she died, and another grave was dug beside Grandfather's.

Father and Mother and the older children tried to make the Christmas season as happy a time as possible for the younger ones, even though they did not feel like celebrating. Each evening the family sang the familiar Advent songs. During the day Mother let everyone who wanted to do so help her bake *lebkuchen* and *springerle* and other Christmas cookies. In the evening after the little children were in bed, she put the older ones to work making Christmas tree decorations out of scraps of brightly-colored yarn.

A few days before Christmas, Father and Johannes went to one of the forests near West Point and cut a small evergreen tree, which they hid from the eyes of the little children by putting it into the wagon.

Then on Christmas Eve, while Mother told the younger children stories in the bedroom, Johannes helped Father decorate the tree, while Susanna and Barbara put a small plate with a few nuts and some of the cookies at each person's place at the table. Then the four of them began to sing the Christmas hymn, "Come hither, you children," which would be the signal to Mother that things were ready for the little ones to see what the Christchild had brought.

After the younger children had enjoyed the Christmas tree and the whole family had played games and sung Christmas songs together, it was time to eat the cookies and then go to bed.

As Susanna snuggled down under the feather bed with Barbara and Katharina that night, she thought, "It was a lovely Christmas after all, our first one here in America, even without Grandfather and Baby Maria."

CHAPTER 12

Soon after Christmas, on December 27, Uncle John Ruth bought a farm on the Franklin Prairie right next to where the John Krehbiels had bought theirs the spring before. He paid $2,235 for 172 acres. The next day Father bought the farm adjoining Uncle John's and also near the Krehbiel farm.

"Ours cost $2,240 for 200 acres," he told the family that evening. "One hundred five acres are fenced and under cultivation, and ninety acres are timberland."

"So the three of us families will be living close to each other again as we did at Eichstock," Mother remarked happily. But she had an important question. "Is there a house on the place?" she wanted to know.

"Yes, there is a house on the place," Father assured her. "It's a one-story brick building with three rooms and a hall."

Mother's next question was, "How soon can we move there?"

Father hesitated, then shrugged his shoulders.

"There is a question about that," he said. "The McQuires are moving to Oregon. Mr. McQuire was willing to sell the farm to me right now so that I can put out some spring crops as soon as the weather allows, but they don't want to move until April when the weather is warmer."

"Not until April?" Mother repeated. "You mean we will have to pay for the farm now, but will have to pay rent to live here until April?"

"I mentioned that to Mr. McQuire," Father said, "and he suggested that we could move now and live with them until they leave."

Mother's face brightened, then she stopped smiling and shook her head.

"You told me that the house is a one story brick house with three rooms and a hall," she said. "I suppose Mrs. McQuire and I can share the kitchen, which will leave a room for each of our families. But can you imagine the nine of us living in one small room?"

Father and Mother stood looking at each other for awhile without either of them saying anything. Then Mother burst out laughing.

"After the three months on the trip we should be used to living in a small space," she said. "And here I can always send the children outside if the house seems too crowded, while on the ship I couldn't very well push them off into the ocean. We'll manage all right. Let's move into our new home as soon as we can."

So the Ruth family moved in with the McQuires. And although Mrs. McQuire knew no German and Mother could neither understand nor speak English, the two got along very well. When the McQuires left for Oregon in late spring, the house seemed empty without them, but everyone in the Ruth family was happy for the extra room.

Susanna had known that here in America, school days would be over for her, as well as for Johannes and Barbara. But that first spring even the younger children in the family could not go to school because there was no school close enough for them to attend.

And soon there would have been little time for school anyway because as soon as the ground had thawed enough, the field work began.

Father had bought a large and a small plow, a harrow, a cradle scythe, and some pitchforks, rakes, and other implements that he would need on the farm from Mr. McQuire. So he felt ready to begin to farm his land.

But his rheumatism was still bothering him so much

that he could hardly walk. Johannes had to do the plowing and harrowing, with Susanna, Barbara, and David helping with the sowing of the wheat and oats.

Later in the spring, for the corn planting, even Katharina and Heinrich were drafted to do their share.

After Johannes had plowed and harrowed the ground, he used a small plow to make a shallow furrow around the field. When he had finished the second round, it was time for David, Katharina, and Heinrich to begin placing the kernels of corn in the cross furrows, while Susanna and Barbara followed them with hoes to cover the seeds and tramp on the spot to push the ground firmly around the kernels.

When it was time to harvest the wheat, Father had to call in help because Johannes was not yet strong enough to swing the cradle. Fortunately, he had no problem finding someone to help him.

Because Mr. Krehbiel had needed to borrow money to buy Jacob's freedom from military service in Germany, in addition to the money needed for the passage to America, he was still heavily in debt. Since so much of the land he had bought in Iowa was forest, he would have little income from his farm until the trees were cut down.

He was renting some additional land for crops, but even so, there was never enough money for the family's needs. So the older boys had to find work to help earn money.

After they had moved to their farm on the Franklin Prairie, Christian's main task had been cutting down trees to clear the forest area. But during the time they had lived in Ohio he had learned how to mow hay with a scythe and cut grain and clover with a cradle scythe. So he was happy to be able to earn some money here in Iowa by doing this kind of work for the Ruths.

As Christian cut the wheat with the cradle, Johannes, Susanna, Barbara, and David raked up the stalks and tied them into bundles with bands of straw, then stacked them together into shocks.

This was not a hard job in the morning right after the wheat had been cut and the straw was still fresh and pliable.

But as the sun rose higher, and the air became hotter and hotter, the stalks began to dry out fast, so that the workers' fingertips became raw from tying the rough bands of straw.

Father had also bought some cows, hogs, and chickens from Mr. McQuire. So milking the cows in the morning and evening was another job which the four oldest of the Ruth children shared. Usually Susanna did not mind this chore. In fact, she found it restful and soothing after a hard days' work in the field. But after tying up wheat bundles all day, milking the cows with her raw, bleeding hands was a very painful job.

When it was time to stack the grain, Father did not need extra help. He had learned from his neighbors how it should be done, and he felt that he had strength enough to do it. Barbara and Johannes gathered the loads of bundles, and Susanna pitched them up to Father on the stack.

Since it took longer to gather the bundles than it did to stack them, Susanna always took along some knitting or sewing to work on while she waited for Barbara and Johannes to bring another load. Keeping up with the sewing, knitting, and mending for the whole family was too much for Mother, and Susanna enjoyed doing it, especially the knitting. She usually brought something to read along to the field, too. She did not need to look at her needles while she knitted, so her eyes could read the book while her hands did the knitting.

Mother had planted a garden near the house, so even when there was no field work, everyone in the family was busy. For Mother, Susanna, and Barbara there was also the cleaning and the laundry and mending. And somehow it all seemed harder to do here on the prairie than it had on their cozy farmyard in Eichstock.

Whenever anyone complained, Mother was quick to say emphatically, "But I'm not sorry that we came to America! I would not have wanted to raise my family in sinful Bavaria!"

There was, of course, no work on Sunday. Even most of the food preparations were made the day before. And, unless the weather was extremely bad, the whole Ruth family went to church.

A number of other Mennonite families were already living on the Franklin Prairie when the Ruths and Krehbiels moved there, and a Mennonite church was being built about four miles from where the Ruths were living. Until it was finished, the Ruths would have liked to continue attending the church near West Point, but the distance was too great. So they did what a number of the other Mennonite families were doing.

The German Evangelical Church had invited the Mennonites to share their building until their own church was built. The Evangelicals held services only every other Sunday, so the Mennonites used the church for their services on the alternate Sundays. But many of them also attended the Evangelical services so that they could go to church every Sunday. And this is what the Ruths did most of the time.

A catechism class was held on the Sundays when the Mennonites had their own services. Susanna attended the class and was baptized in the Evangelical church in the spring.

Even though the arrangement with the Evangelicals was working out quite well, all of the Mennonite families were glad when their own church building was finished. At the dedication services they named it the Zion Mennonite Church. Set in a grove of evergreen trees, it was a well-planned, well-built wooden church with a schoolroom at one end of the basement.

Susanna was happy that Father was asked to be one of the ministers at the new church. Henry Ellenberger, the minister she had learned to know and like at the West Point church, was another one of the ministers. So were Jacob Krehbiel and Jacob Schnebele. The new teacher was Christian Schowalter, who had been teaching in a Mennonite school in Ohio.

Susanna envied David, Katharina and Heinrich, who would now be going to school regularly. Mr. Schowalter looked like he would be a kind, helpful teacher, and the new schoolroom would be a nice place to study. But she knew that her school days were over.

Since the church was three miles from their farm, the Ruths usually rode to church in the farm wagon. But when the road was not in good enough condition to use a wagon, which happened often when it rained or snowed, those who wanted to go to church had to walk. Father could not walk that far, so he bought himself an old nag, which he rode in bad weather while the rest of the family walked.

In some ways Susanna enjoyed the Sundays when they walked more than when they rode in the wagon. There was something about walking through the lovely forest that made it seem almost like a part of the worship service.

That summer passed quickly and soon it was autumn. In October something happened which kept Susanna and Barbara busy in the house instead of in the fields. When the children woke up on the morning of October 4, Mother was still in bed, and beside her lay a tiny new baby.

"It's a boy," Father said happily, and Mother added, "He's a strong, healthy little fellow!"

The little newcomer was named Gerhard Benjamin, and although he could never take the place of Baby Maria in their hearts, he did help to fill the vacant spot in the family that Maria's death had left.

As soon as the weather turned really cold, another job brought Christian Krehbiel to the Ruth home.

Many of the farmers on the Franklin Prairie raised large herds of hogs which were butchered in the winter. The lard was rendered, the meat was salted down, then it was all stored in barrels. The families kept what they thought they would need, and the rest was taken to the market in St. Louis.

When he was still living in Germany, Christian had learned the butcher's trade from an uncle. So now he was in great demand as a master butcher.

Father had bought some hogs, in addition to those he had raised, so that he would have more lard and meat to sell. One icy cold morning Christian came for the butchering.

When they had been neighbors in Bavaria, Christian had simply been one of the Krehbiel boys to Susanna. But watching him take care of Grandfather Strohm in West Point, she had found herself admiring him as someone special. And as they worked together in the wheat fields, she and Christian had learned to know each other very well.

Now, as she looked out of the window and watched him cut up and clean the carcasses in the freezing weather, she found herself thinking, Not many young men would be willing to do this kind of work day after day. And he's doing it to earn money for his family, not for himself.

Later, as she watched him render the lard and make sausage in the crowded kitchen, she marveled at the skill with which he did it.

He works so fast, she thought, and yet he seems to do everything just right.

It was almost midnight before Christian was ready to leave. Susanna was so tired that she felt ready to fall asleep on her feet.

"Tomorrow I go to Uncle Kramer's," Christian told Father as he pulled on his coat and stocking cap. "I'll have to get an early start because he has almost twice as many hogs to butcher as you had."

As she lay snuggled under the featherbed, Susanna found herself still thinking about Christian, wondering whether he was already at home and in bed, too.

Soon after butchering time was over, preparations for Christmas began. There was the usual baking of Christmas cookies and the special cleaning of the house. Then, after what seemed a long time to wait, it was time for the Christmas Eve celebration at home and the Christmas morning services at the new church.

And then it was New Year. The second year in their new home began for the Ruths.

Chapter 13

Susanna walked slowly up the stairs to her bedroom, so tired from the day's work that she could hardly drag her feet from one step to the other.

She had been here at Denmark, eighteen miles from home, for more than two months now, doing housework for their former English neighbors, the Clark family. When Mr. Clark had asked Susanna to come along with them when they moved, and work for his wife, Susanna had not wanted to go. She felt very shy with people whom she did not know well, and she knew very few English words.

But Mother and Father had thought it would be a good way for her to learn more English as well as to earn some money.

Susanna knew that Father was having trouble meeting all of the expenses of the family even though the crops had been quite good for several years. Barbara had been working for a family in West Point all winter, and wanted to rest at home for a while before going to work again. So it had been only fair that Susanna take her turn leaving home to go to work.

The young woman for whom Susanna was working was Mr. Clark's third wife. There were four children in the family when Susanna came. The youngest, a three-year-old boy, was the son of Mr. Clark's second wife. The older three were children of his first wife. Soon after Susanna started to work for the family another baby was born.

Mr. Clark was a farmer, who also had a large herd of cows. Susanna did not have to help milk the cows, but she had to take care of the milk and make the butter. She also had to do all of the housework alone—the cooking and baking, the spring house cleaning, and the laundry.

Before she could wash the clothes she had to draw the water from the well and carry it across a long yard in a bucket, then heat it on a wood-burning stove. And after the clothes were clean, they had to be hung on a line outdoors. And there were always a number of things that Mrs. Clark wanted to have ironed.

For all of this work Susanna was being paid five dollars a month.

Today had been an especially busy day! In addition to the regular Saturday work, Susanna had done some extra cooking and baking so that the Clark family would have enough to eat while she was gone.

Tomorrow, on Sunday, Susanna would have a chance to go home for the first time since she had come to work for the Clarks. A family who lived near the Clarks was going to visit relatives who lived near the Ruth farm, and they had invited Susanna to go along and visit her family. Mrs. Clark had been hesitant at first about giving Susanna the day off, but she had grudgingly given her consent.

"How I wish I could bring a lamp up here with me so that the room wouldn't be so completely dark," Susanna thought as she undressed quickly and slipped into bed.

Her body was exhausted, but her mind was restless. It would be nice to be able to relax by reading a while. That was one of the things she missed most since she had been working for the Clarks. She had no time to read. As long as she stayed downstairs in the evening she was expected to sew or mend things for the family. And Mrs. Clark would not allow her to take a lamp upstairs.

As she lay thinking about her family and how wonderful it would be to see all of them, Susanna found her mind going back to things that had happened in the past.

It was four years now since the family had come to

America. Sometimes it seemed to Susanna that the trip to Iowa had happened only a short time ago. But most of the time it seemed as though they had always been living here, and that Eichstock was only a dream. Life had settled into a familiar, pleasant pattern, with one month seeming to merge into the next one more and more quickly. There had been some unhappy times. Last year in November another brother, Christian, was born. He had not seemed as strong as little Gerhard had been, and as time went by, he had grown weaker instead of stronger. When he was six weeks old, he died, leaving another empty spot in the family.

Shortly after that another sad thing had happened which affected Susanna even more than little Christian's death had.

Uncle John Ruth had died. Since the two families had lived in one house in Eichstock, he had seemed almost like a second father to Susanna, and his death had affected her so strongly that she had gone through a period of real soul searching. She had felt as if the sun had stopped shining—everything had seemed dark, and nothing had seemed worthwhile for a time, and she still felt depressed when she thought about Uncle's death.

There had been many busy times!

One of the busiest for Susanna and Barbara had been last summer. Father had bought a McCormick reaper, the first one in the area. It worked a little like a hay cutting machine. The blades cut the stalks of grain, which then fell onto a platform where a man stood and raked the stalks of grain off onto the ground. There it was bound and then shocked.

Father had driven the horses that pulled the machine and Johannes had raked the grain off the platform. When the neighbors saw how it worked, many of them had wanted Father to cut their grain. Since the machine had cost $167, Father had been only too happy to be able to earn some money with it. So he had cut for several of the neighbors and had earned forty-eight dollars.

Since Father and Johannes had been busy working for the neighbors, the job of binding the grain and shocking it had fallen to Susanna and Barbara. The straw had been so dry and sharp and the bands which were now being used to tie the bundles had been so hard to tie that Susanna's hands had hurt more by evening than they had with the old way of tying, using wheat stalks.

But not all of life since they had come to America had been unhappiness and hard work. There had also been some special happy occasions!

One spring, after Susanna had helped in the Kramer home during the hog-butchering time, Uncle Kramer had invited her to go along with him, his stepdaughter, and a friend, to visit Uncle and Aunt Leisy at Summerfield, Illinois.

Susanna had hardly been able to believe her eyes when she saw Uncle Leisy's farm. He had a two-story brick house, a large barn, and several granaries for his wheat, oats, and corn. The peach, apricot, apple, cherry, and plum trees in the large orchard behind the house had been loaded with fruit, and Aunt Leisy's garden had been much bigger than Mother's.

When Susanna had told Father about all of this after she got home, Father had nodded his head, then said sadly, "Yes, the land there is rich loam, which is much better for wheat and corn and fruit trees than the soil here on the Franklin Prairie. But the price of land is also much higher there than it is here. I would not have had money enough to buy land in Illinois, but perhaps, if we continue to do well here and can save some money, we can still move to Illinois some time."

Thinking about the trip to Illinois after having helped in Uncle Kramer's home during butchering time reminded Susanna of Christian Krehbiel, who had also helped with the butchering. And thinking about Christian filled her with a warm, happy feeling.

She felt her body relax, and when she closed her eyes she began to feel drowsy. Then the next thing of which she was aware was the sound of Mrs. Clark's broom handle tapping on the ceiling downstairs to let Susanna know that it was time to get up.

After breakfast Susanna barely had time to hurriedly wash the dishes before a wagon drove into the Clark yard to pick her up for the ride home. But then time seemed to drag as she rode in the neighbor's wagon to the place south of West Point where Susanna got off to walk the rest of the way home.

Susanna had not been able to let her family know that she was coming, so her visit took them completely by surprise. For a while there was bedlam in the room as Mother and Father and all of the brothers and sisters greeted and hugged her. After they were all seated at the table and grace had been said, Mother sat looking at Susanna, then shook her head.

"My dear girl!" she said, "What in the world has happened to you? You look so thin and tired. Have you been sick?"

"No, I haven't been sick, but I have been working very hard," Susanna told her. Then she found herself bursting into tears.

When she got control of herself enough so that she could talk, Susanna told the family about all of the work she had been expected to do.

"You are not going back there again to work!" Mother said emphatically when Susanna had finished. "You may not be sick now, but I'm afraid you will be if you have to work that hard much longer. Perhaps Barbara can go for a few weeks until the woman can find someone else."

Barbara reluctantly consented to go, but she did not stay long. She was used to working for considerate women, so as soon as she could, she came back home.

Mother did not scold her. "I'll be happy to have both you and Susanna at home right now," she said with a smile. "I haven't been feeling well for several days, and I think I may be pregnant again. So I'll just be lazy and rest much of each day and let the two of you manage the household."

Barbara and Susanna looked at each other in concern, and Mother laughed.

"Don't worry," she reassured them. "I'll be all right. I've gone through this a few times before. But it will be nice to have you both at home to do the heavy work and keep an eye on little Gerhard."

For Susanna the months that followed were the most enjoyable and relaxing time she had experienced for years.

80

Both she and Barbara helped in the field, but only during wheat harvest time, and Susanna was so glad to be at home again that she did not even mind when her hands got sore from binding the wheat into bundles.

Most of the summer in addition to the regular housework of cooking, baking, laundry, and cleaning, Susanna had time to do the things she enjoyed: sewing, mending, and gardening. And in the evening she could knit and read.

The baby, a little girl, was born on August 27. She was named Maria Amalia in memory of the Maria who had died, but all of the family soon called her "Malchen."

Chapter 14

It was early on a Sunday morning. The sun had not yet risen, but glowing clouds in the eastern sky showed Susanna that sunrise was not far away. She was walking through the woods on their farm, looking for their cows, which had been turned into the woods the evening before, as they were every evening and again in the morning after the milking.

The grass grew lush here in the woods, and Father's eighty acres of woodland joined that of Uncle John's and Mr. Krehbiel's, so the cows had all the pasture they wanted. Each family's herd had its own bell, which could be heard from far away, so each family could listen and know where their own cows were feeding.

Susanna had some time ago spotted the sound of the Ruth bell, and as she walked toward it she thought about her cow herding days in the Eichstock meadow and one of the reasons she had wanted to come to America.

"In America one does not have to herd the cows," she said out loud with a chuckle. "One has to hunt them!"

By now Susanna was far into the forest, standing on a slight rise where she could look over the edge of the hillside. The sun was rising. The fall flowers and the leaves of the crabapple and plum trees, which had turned red and golden and yellow, sparkled in the morning dew.

Not far away, on a lower level, Susanna could see the forty-acre patch of woods where she and Christian Krehbiel had paused several weeks before as they were walking from Christian's home to the Ruth's.

"If this land, and you, were mine," Christian had said, I could wish for nothing more. I would build us a log house and would work for our living."

"He does not yet own the woodland, and perhaps he never will. But I will soon be his!" Susanna thought happily.

Christian had proposed to Susanna that afternoon, and she had shyly let him know what he no doubt had already guessed, that she would like to be his wife.

The next evening Christian had come over to talk to Mother and Father about it, and they had given their consent to the marriage. Several Sundays later Mother had invited the Krehbiel family over for the Sunday noon meal. In the afternoon Susanna and Christian and the parents had made plans for the wedding, and for Susanna and Christian's future.

Some years earlier Father had built a little one-room stone house near the Ruth's home, and it was decided that this was where Susanna and Christian would live. They would both work for Father and Mother, who would pay them $140 a year.

So everything was settled for the future.

As Susanna turned again toward the sound of the cowbells, a warm glow of happiness and contentment flooded over her. Life in her wonderland might not always be easy, but it was good, with the promise of even greater happiness ahead!

The wedding date was set for March 7.

Before he moved from his home, Christian wanted to do some carpentry, fence building, and other work for his father, who was not well. His older brother, Jacob, had married two years before, and was living near Summerfield, Illinois, and the other boys were still too young to do this kind of work.

When he could not get all of this finished by the set date, the wedding was postponed until March 14.

Susanna woke up early that morning. Slipping out of bed, she walked over to the window.

We'll have a beautiful day, she thought happily. The air

felt like a typical spring day, warm enough to draw the winter frost out of the ground.

Then, as she watched some clouds scudding across the sky, she added, "If it does not rain."

The clouds did drop some of their moisture on the Ruth family as they drove to the church in the farm wagon with umbrellas spread over them. "But by noon the sky should be bright and clear," Father said reassuringly.

All of the members of the Zion church, as well as friends and relatives from the West Point church, had been invited to the wedding. So the sanctuary was filled as Susanna walked with Christian down the aisle to sit on the special wedding chairs at the front of the church. Christian seemed calm and relaxed, but Susanna felt shy and uncomfortable at the thought of so many eyes watching her.

Christian's uncle, Jacob Krehbiel II, preached a short sermon, and performed the wedding ceremony, ending with some words of admonition to Christian and Susanna and a prayer for their life together. Then it was time for the two of them to walk together to the back of the church and be congratulated by family and friends.

Susanna still felt shy as she walked down the aisle to the back of the church with Christian's hand holding her arm, but she nodded and smiled at the people who were smiling at her, just as Christian was doing. And later in the church yard when friends and relatives crowded around them to shake hands and to congratulate her and Christian, she began to relax and to enjoy all of the attention she was getting.

A number of relatives and young friends had been invited to the wedding dinner at noon, and most of them stayed for an afternoon of visiting. It was a relaxed and happy time, and Susanna enjoyed it. But as she and Christian walked to their little home after the guests had gone home, she found herself still thinking about something that had been bothering her.

As she and Christian were getting up from the dinner table, he had said to her, "You must not expect me to devote myself to you alone today. I belong to the guests as well."

The remark hurt Susanna's feelings!

Why would Christian think that she would be so self-centered and selfish that she would want him to pay attention only to her? On the other hand, this was their special day together. Why would he not want to be with her as much as possible? Why couldn't they "belong to the guests" together?

She found herself thinking about the remark all afternoon, and she still could not get it out of her mind.

But after they got to their little home, no one could have been more loving and considerate than Christian was. And when they knelt beside their bed before going to sleep, and Christian prayed earnestly for God's blessing on their life together, all the hurt of the afternoon vanished for Susanna.

Life soon settled into a happy, familiar routine for Susanna. Since she, as well as Christian, was working for Father and Mother now, Susanna's daily routine of chores and housework was not much different than it had been before her marriage. But there were always the evenings when she and Christian were alone together that were different and special.

And so was the feeling that this was her own home, hers and Christian's alone!

Father and Mother had given them a bed and a clothes cupboard, and Christian had brought a large German chest from his home. After Christian had made a wooden sink for them, then a kitchen cupboard, they had everything that they needed or wanted and Susanna had never felt more contented in all of her life.

Then something happened that changed Susanna's happy, contented feeling into frightened concern.

One morning Christian complained of his eyes hurting. He went to work as usual, but at dinnertime Susanna noticed that they were red and watering. And instead of laughing and joking and talking with the rest of the family as he usually did, Christian sat quietly with a pained look on his face, and when he went out into the sunlight, Susanna noticed that he shaded his eyes with his hand.

So she was not surprised when he came back to the house from the field to tell her that Father had sent him home to get out of the sun. By now his eyes were red and watering, and Mother expressed her concern that he might have some sort of infection.

By the next morning his eyes were so inflamed and painful that there was no question of Christian going to work. The shades in the little house stayed closed all day, and when Susanna came home she found Christian walking back and forth in the dark hallway, in too much anguish to sit or lie still. Even at night he slept only restlessly.

By the next morning the pain was worse instead of better. And when Susanna came home again at noon to check on him he was again pacing the floor in too much pain to sit still. And so it continued day after day and week after week!

"The thing that is hardest for me to bear," Christian told Susanna repeatedly, "is the thought that I will lose my eyesight and become a burden to you."

Then one day Susanna came home from helping Mother with her work to find Christian sitting calmly in a chair, his hands over his eyes, singing softly to himself the familiar hymn, *"Was Gott tut, das ist wohlgetan, Es bleibt gerecht sein Wille"* (Whatever my God ordains is right; his holy will abideth).

"I have finally been able to resign myself to the will of God," he told Susanna calmly. "I am able to say that if I do become blind, I will be guided by him."

Gradually, very gradually, Christian's pain became less severe, and by the end of the month it had almost gone away. His eyesight was still so poor that he could not see more than a hundred yards, but he was able to begin to do some work on the farm again.

Soon after that it was Susanna's turn to feel sick. When she got up one morning, she felt so nauseated that she lay down on the bed again. But she did not stay down long. She knew she was going to vomit, and she did not want to soil the bedding. By hurrying, she got outside the house before the vomit came.

Christian, who had followed her out, put his arm around her, steadying her until she was through, then wiped her mouth with his handkerchief.

When she looked up to thank him she was surprised to see him smiling happily.

"Go on up to your parents' house and talk to your Mother," he said, giving her a hug. "She'll be able to tell you what to do. She no doubt had the same problem about a year and a half ago."

A year and a half ago? That was about the time that Mother had told Susanna and Barbara that she thought she was "with child" again.

"I'm pregnant!" she thought happily, returning Christian's hug. She had thought that she was completely happy being Christian's wife. But to become the mother of his child—that would make their happiness complete!

"Mother was happy to have another girl when little Amalia was born," she told Christian. "But perhaps I can give you a little son."

"It does not matter," Christian assured her.

"Let's go talk to Mother," she told Christian, taking his hand. As they walked together to her parents' home, Susanna found herself thinking, "Wonderful, wonderful wonderland!"

Life here in America had not always been as happy and easy as she had thought it would be when she was a young girl in Bavaria. But it had been good, and now it would be even better!

CHAPTER 15

The new year, 1859, began as other years had. But soon Susanna found many things in her life changing.

For one thing, her brothers and sisters were growing up, and the family was beginning to scatter.

In October, Aunt Barbara Kramer, Father's sister, had come from Summerfield for a four-week visit. When she went home, Susanna's brother David, and Uncle John Ruth's son, Daniel, had gone with her to learn the cabinet making trade in Illinois. Barbara was away from home much of the time working for various families, and she and David Lehman were making plans to get married soon.

Christian and Susanna's baby was born during the night of February 19. She and Christian were all alone in their little home. Susanna had a chance to find out again how skillful Christian was as a nurse, and how loving he was as a husband. After the baby was born and Christian had taken care of everything, little David was lying beside Susanna in the bed. Christian knelt beside the bed. He thanked God for his son, then entrusted mother and child to God's care.

In the days that followed, Susanna marveled at Christian's ability to do the housework and to cook. Mother came back and forth from her house to give advice and to help, but she could not stay long. Barbara was working for another family, the older children were in school, and little Amalia was at the age where she could not be left alone.

Soon after Susanna was able to be up and to do her own work again, life changed even more for her. Father's rheumatism continued to bother him, and he was having other health problems. So he decided to rent his farm to Christian and Susanna's brother John.

John moved into the little stone house with Susanna and Christian. Instead of working for Mother and eating her meals at her parents' home, Susanna had to establish her own household with four people in it.

Christian had become more and more active in the work of the Zion church, where his Uncle Jacob Krehbiel was one of the ministers. He was enthusiastic about the plans being made by the leaders of the Zion church and the West Point church to organize a General Conference. This conference would include all the Mennonite churches in America.

"It will be like the organizations we had in Bavaria and the Palatinate in Germany," he told Susanna. "Daniel Krehbiel was the originator of the idea. The other church leaders here in Iowa, as well as those in Summerfield, Illinois, are interested in it, too. They are planning to have a meeting on March 21 in our church."

Father was as enthusiastic about the idea of organizing a conference as Christian was. As one of the ministers at Zion, he was helping to make the plans. He often discussed them with Christian.

"One purpose of the conference," he said one day when he was talking to Christian, "will be to unite the Mennonite churches here in America. But the main purpose is to have the churches work together in supporting and carrying out mission work. We want to minister to the isolated families in Missouri and other places, and do mission work among the Indians."

When the conference met in March, Christian attended each of the sessions. In the evening he enthusiastically reported to Susanna what had happened.

"Jacob Krehbiel III of our Zion church made the motion to invite all of the Mennonite churches in Ohio, Illinois, and the eastern states to take part in a meeting a year from now," he told her. "He and all the others who are attending the conference feel that if we work together we can carry out missionary work much more successfully."

"One of the resolutions was to send my uncle, Jacob Krehbiel II to Oskaloosa, Iowa, to preach the gospel to the Mennonites living there and to administer the sacrament of the Lord's Supper," he went on. "Daniel Krehbiel and Jacob Ellenberger of the West Point church and Jacob Krehbiel I and Jacob Krehbiel III of our Zion church were elected to serve as the business committee for our union. Plans were made to hold the meeting at Wadsworth, Ohio, on May 28 and 29 in 1860."

"It all sounds so interesting," Susanna thought as she tried to keep little David happy, get supper ready, and listen to Christian at the same time. Sometimes she wished she were a man so that she could take part in such things as the conference that Christian was describing.

As soon as the conference was over, Christian and Father again began to talk about something they had discussed frequently all winter.

Christian's older brother, Jacob, had been living in Illinois since his marriage. He seemed to be doing well in his farming. So Christian had for some time been interested in moving there. As for Father, each time he visited Uncle Leisy, he came back to Iowa making comparisons between his own farm and Uncle Leisy's prosperous one at Summerfield.

Christian was not satisfied to continue renting Father's farm with John for any length of time. Barbara and David Lehman from Ohio were planning to be married soon. They would also need a place to live.

Father had been able to save some money each year for several years. In early March he had gone to Illinois with the intention of buying a farm, but instead had bought four lots in Summerfield for $140. He had talked to Uncle Leisy about an eighty-acre farm one and a half miles east of Summerfield that was for sale for $3,150.

"I think you should go to Illinois and look at the farm," Father told Christian. "You can have a visit with your brother while you are there. Talk to Uncle Leisy. Then use your own judgment about buying the land and making arrangements about the payments."

It was the first time since they were married that Christian had been gone for the night. Susanna realized how dependent on him she had become. Even little David seemed to miss his father in the evenings, and did not want to settle down and go to sleep for the night. Susanna was glad that John was there so she was not all alone with the baby.

When Christian returned he reported to Susanna and Father that he thought the conditions that Uncle Leisy had suggested were good, so definite plans were made to buy the land. The $3,150 could be paid in three installments, the first one due in the fall.

Father let Uncle Leisy know by mail that he wanted to buy the land and would make a payment of $1,000 in November. Definite plans were made for the move to Illinois.

Christian had been concerned about leaving his parents, since his Father was not at all well. When his father became critically ill in the summer, plans for the move were temporarily postponed.

Instead of getting better during the summer and fall, Mr. Krehbiel continued to get worse. There was no doctor closer than thirty miles away, and there was not enough money to ask a doctor to come from there. So Mr. Krehbiel was nursed by members of the family who watched him grow weaker and weaker until he passed away a week before Christmas.

"He was only sixty years old," Christian's mother said sadly. "He should have had a number of good years with us yet."

When Christian's older brother Jacob invited his mother and youngest brothers to come and live with him in Illinois, Susanna and Christian also began to make definite plans to move without any more delay. After Barbara and David Lehman were married on February 26, 1860, the date for the two couples to move to Illinois was set for March 13.

Mother and the younger children went along in the wagon when Father took the two couples to the place where they would board the steamer docked in the Mississippi River. The ride reminded Susanna of the day the family had left

Eichstock to come to America.

At that time she had felt eager to go to the wonderland, but still unhappy about leaving her Eichstock home. Now she was eager to live in Illinois, happy that she and Christian would have their own home and farm. She was glad to be able to visit the Illinois friends and relatives often.

But one part of her still wanted to stay safely at home in Iowa. She wanted to be able to go to Mother for advice and encouragement, to be with her friends at church on Sundays, and to watch little Malchen grow up day by day.

She wished she could be as eager for new experiences and adventures as Christian was. Holding little David, he was standing beside Barbara and David Lehman at the railing. They were laughing and talking as they watched the steamer leave the Iowa shore further and further behind.

Looking at Christian's happy face as he watched the countryside go by, Susanna was reminded of the afternoon when she had come home to find him singing instead of pacing the floor because of the pain in his eyes. The words of the song he was singing at that time began to sing themselves in her mind: "Whatever my God ordains is right; his holy will abideth."

Christian and she had often prayed about their future plans. This move to Illinois seemed to be the answer.

"Whatever my God ordains is right," she said softly to herself as she walked over to the railing to stand beside Christian.

CHAPTER 16

When Susanna thought about living in Illinois she had remembered Uncle Leisy's lovely farm with the large brick house, the big barns, the grassy lawn, the orchard and garden.

And during their first days in Illinois, while Christian and David were busy buying horses and wagons and other equipment that they would need on their farm, Susanna and Barbara enjoyed visiting with Aunt Leisy in her spacious, comfortable home. So, on the morning when they went out to the farm where they would live, she was not prepared for what she saw when Christian drove the wagon up a long lane and stopped the horses.

"Here we are," he said cheerfully as he climbed out of the wagon. He lifted little David from Susanna's lap, then held out his other hand to help her down. "Here we are at our new home!"

What Susanna saw as she looked around her was not anything like what she had expected to see.

There were three buildings on the place—a small barn, an even smaller machine shed, and a house, with weeds and high grass growing between them.

Barbara and David Lehman got out of their wagon, too, and Barbara came to stand beside Susanna.

"Looks like nobody has lived here for some time," she commented. It's going to take some hard work to clean up the place."

"Yes, it is!" Susanna agreed emphatically, then added,

knowing that Barbara would recognize the remark as a quote from Mother, "But all beginning is difficult."

Christian handed little David back to Susanna. "Why don't you and Barbara go and see what the house is like inside," he suggested. We'll put the horses into the barn and get the furniture unloaded."

When Barbara and Susanna got close to the house, they realized that it wasn't one house. There were two small one room houses built very close together, so that they touched each other. One of the houses was very small and looked quite old.

"It's probably the one in which the people lived first," Barbara commented. "And when they built the new one they just left the old one there. Let's go into the newer one first."

This house had only one room, but the walls and the floor were in good condition. And after the small one-room stone house in which she and Christian had been living since their marriage, Susanna thought it looked quite spacious.

When they were ready to go into the other house, the women realized that there was no door between the two houses.

"So we'll have to go outside to get from one of our rooms to the other," Barbara chuckled.

By the time the men had unloaded the furniture and carried some of it to the house, Susanna and Barbara had made their plans. Although the small house was in poor condition, with the floor rough and splintery, the chimney seemed to be well built and in good condition.

"We'll use the old house for our kitchen and dining room," they told the men. "Then the other one can be our bedroom and living room."

By the time the men had brought the furniture into the house and arranged it, then checked on the horses, it was getting dark. The cooking stove had been set up in the small house, but Christian wanted to check the chimney before he connected the stove pipes to it. So the women decided it would be best just to eat a quick meal of bread and cheese and then get ready for bed.

As Susanna lay in bed that night with little David sleeping peacefully in his cradle nearby and Christian already dropping off to sleep, she began to feel relaxed and content.

"I'll probably be homesick for Mother and Father and my Iowa friends," she thought, "but I'll have Barbara to help me cope with things, and it will feel good to have our own home and farm."

They had come to the farm on a Saturday, so the next morning everyone got up early so the men could do the chores while the women got breakfast and everyone would be ready to leave for church on time.

Susanna had been disappointed in their farm home, but their first Sunday worshiping with the Mennonite congregation at Summerfield made her feel good about having moved to Illinois. Although she was acquainted with only a few of the people attending the services, she found everyone to be so friendly that she knew she would soon feel at home with the church group.

Uncle and Aunt Leisy invited them for dinner and the afternoon. Then, when she found out that the cookstove was not yet set up, Aunt Leisy sent some food along with them for the evening meal.

The next morning the men finished setting up the cooking stove in the small house and helped Barbara and Susanna rearrange the furniture in the other house. Then they went to check on the forty acres of wheat that Christian's brother Jakob had planted for them. When they came back a short time later, the expression on Christian's face warned Susanna that something was wrong.

"Well," she said, "What does the wheat look like?"

It was David who answered. "There isn't any wheat. Not a sign of any wheat growing. It must have completely frozen out during the winter."

"You mean we won't have a wheat crop to harvest?" Barbara asked. "So what will we do to get money to live on?"

"Oh," Christian said, shrugging his shoulders, "It's not too late to plant corn. Of course, it won't be the cash crop that the wheat would have been, but it will be worth something."

After the corn was all planted, the men plowed and harrowed some ground near the house to use as a garden. Susanna and Barbara planted all of the kinds of vegetables that Mother had always planted in Iowa, and to their delight everything grew well. By early summer they had more lettuce, spinach, tomatoes, carrots, peas, and beans than they could use.

"If we could sell some of these, we could get some much needed cash," Christian remarked one day when he saw how many peas the women had picked.

"Well, why can't we?" Barbara responded. "There should be a market for fresh vegetables in town."

"Probably not in Summerfield," Christian said. "Most people there have their own gardens. But perhaps at Trenton."

When Barbara found out that one of their close neighbors went to Trenton often, she made arrangements to go along. To her delight, she was able to sell all of the vegetables that she had taken along, getting a good price for them.

"And the Hirschlers said I could go along each time they go," she reported when she got home. "So we'll have a little cash all spring and summer if our garden continues to do as well as it has been doing."

Life began to settle into a familiar pleasant routine for Susanna. During the week all of them were busy with the work that needed to be done. But the Sundays were days for worship, rest, and relaxation.

They had received a warm welcome from the Summerfield congregation, and by now Susanna felt at home there and no longer missed her West Point friends as much as she had at first. But they had not yet been able to join the church.

Each family attending the church had come from a different congregation in Europe, so they had not yet established a definite organization. But not long after the Krehbiels and Lehmans had moved to Illinois a resolution was passed by those who had been attending the church that any Mennonite man or woman who signed the membership roll would be a member, regardless of their previous home or past church record. But only those who signed would be members. Women could not sign, but a minister could sign for them upon their request.

So Christian and David signed the roll and Susanna and Barbara asked the minister, Daniel Hirschler, to sign for them. So all four of them had become members of the Summerfield Mennonite Church.

Susanna was pregnant again, and as the weather became warmer and warmer she began to feel more and more miserable. So she was happy when the baby was born on August 10, 1860.

It was another boy, whom they named John after Susanna's older brother. This time Susanna did not regain her strength as fast as after David's birth. So she was glad that Barbara was there to help her care for the baby.

"I'll just claim him as mine," Barbara chuckled as she bathed the little boy and laid him into the cradle, "at least until my own arrives."

When little John was a few weeks old something happened that reminded Susanna and Barbara of their first weeks in Iowa right after they had come from Germany. Both of the men became sick with the ague.

So, besides taking care of the little boys and nursing the sick men, Barbara and Susanna had to do the chores. Aunt Leisy had given Barbara and Susanna each a young cow with calf as a gift when they first came to Illinois, and Christian had bought a somewhat older cow.

So there were three cows to milk and feed twice a day, as well as feeding the hogs and the horses.

None of the remedies prescribed for the ague seemed to give a permanent cure. Each time that the men thought they were feeling better, the fever returned. One day when Christian had gone to work on the road, Susanna happened to look out of the door shortly before noon and saw Christian's wagon standing at the gate, but there was no sign of him.

When she went out to check on things, Susanna found Christian lying unconscious in the wagon box. She called

Barbara, and the two of them managed to carry him into the house and put him onto a bed. But it took several hours before he regained consciousness. And even by the next morning he did not feel well enough to get out of bed.

Needless to say, all of them were happy when cold weather set in and both men recovered from the ague. But the cold weather brought other problems.

The little house was not warm enough to be used during the winter. Even when there was a good fire burning in the cooking stove, the cold draft that came in through the floor and the cracks in the wall, made it very uncomfortable for anyone to stay in the room for any length of time. So the stove and all of the other kitchen furniture had to be moved into the other house.

The table was set up between the beds, which were then used to sit on, especially when company came and there were not enough chairs for everyone.

When the weather turned colder and colder the horses had to be fed in the barn instead of simply being turned out to graze in the pasture. Since they had no hay, Christian and David had raised some millet for horse feed, but it was full of seeds, and did not seem to agree with the horses. They became fat and shiny, then suddenly they were lame, and then really sick.

As he had done when he was living in Iowa, Christian spent many of the winter days slaughtering hogs for friends and neighbors, and often he did not even come home for the night. So it was Susanna who had to be the horse doctor, in addition to her other responsibilities. Fortunately, their horses both recovered. But both of the Lehman's horses died.

The Lehman's son, Chris, was born on March 25, 1861. Now it was Susanna's turn to be the nurse and take care of the mother and baby, as well as looking after her two little boys. There were two cradles in the one room in addition to little David's trundle bed and all of the other furniture.

And Susanna and Barbara began to look forward to warm weather so that they could move some of the furniture back to the little house, just as they had looked forward to colder weather when the men were sick with the ague.

But before that time came, something else happened that changed life for all of them.

Susanna and Barbara had both realized for some time that their husbands would not be satisfied for any length of time to farm the small acreage together. So Susanna was not surprised when Christian asked her one evening after he had been helping Uncle Leisy with butchering, "How would you like to move to a farm next to Uncle Leisy's farm?"

Before Susanna could answer, he went on, "Today I met a Prussian by the name of Juergen Reimer who has been traveling across America. He bought a farm next to Uncle Leisy's, but knows nothing about farming. So he's looking for someone to rent his farm with the understanding that he can live with them and work for them."

Although Susanna knew she would miss Barbara's companionship and her help with the two little boys, she didn't have to think twice before she answered, "If you think that is best for us, I'll be willing and happy to move."

CHAPTER 17

Since Christian wanted to help David with the harvest on the place where they were now living, but wanted to be settled in their new home before the time when he would be helping others with their threshing in the fall and butchering in the winter, they decided to move in August.

For both David and Christian there was one problem with dissolving their partnership in farming. Each of them would need to buy more horses.

David had some financial help from his father, so he went to Iowa and bought a pair of mules. Since horses were cheaper in Iowa than in Illinois, Christian also went to Iowa to buy a horse.

When Christian came home, Susanna noticed that the horse he had bought was limping.

"He didn't like the idea of getting onto the boat," Christian explained, "and he struggled enough so that he hurt his leg. We'll hope it will heal before harvest time."

Christian doctored the horse faithfully for many weeks, but it wasn't until just before harvest time that he was well enough to do any work. Then, when Christian started to cut the wheat, something even worse happened.

He began cutting in the orchard where wheat had been sown in order to use all available land. When Susanna saw him bringing the horses back to the barnyard a few minutes later, she went outside to see what was the matter.

"The person who cut the wheat last year with a cradle left it lying in the orchard," Christian told her. "It was hidden enough by the wheat that I didn't notice it until it got caught in the horses' feet. I stopped them as fast as I could, but one of them has a bad cut between the ribs, and some other flesh wounds. Could you find something we could use for bandages to stop the flow of blood?"

Susanna tore up an old sheet and helped Christian bandage the horse's wounds. She changed the bandages faithfully each day, and for a time it seemed to her that the wounds were beginning to heal and the horse was feeling better.

Then, suddenly, about a week later, the horse died. Christian performed an autopsy and found that there was a cut into the stomach and another in the lung.

"So he didn't really have a chance to recover, no matter how well you took care of him," Christian said sadly. "He was hurt too seriously. But now we'll have to find some way to get another horse to replace him."

During the next weeks Susanna felt so depressed that not even taking care of her little boys made her feel any better.

"What will become of us." she kept thinking, "What will we do? The horse wasn't even paid for yet when he died, and now we'll have to buy another one. And how will we manage that when we're already so deeply in debt?"

One evening when Christian came into the house after he had gone to see a farmer who had horses for sale, Susanna couldn't hide the fact that she had been crying much of the afternoon.

"Don't worry so," Christian told her as he put his arm around her. "Even if we lose all of our horses, we'll still get rich some day!"

Then, when Susanna found herself laughing at such a ridiculous statement, Christian held her at arms' length and added, "And I want you to know that I have good news for you. I found two horses today that I can buy at a low price. One of them is quite old, but still strong and healthy; the other one is blind. By putting those two together I'll have a good inexpensive team. And the owner told me, "One can safely sell horses on credit to someone who works as hard as you do."

So the horse problem was solved. But that fall Susanna found herself with more important worries than horses.

Little John caught the children's cholera. He was very sick for a number of weeks and Susanna began to try to reconcile herself to the fact that he might die.

"Oh Heavenly Father," she prayed almost constantly, "Your will be done. But please help our little son to get well."

When cold weather set in, John recovered quickly, and Susanna's prayers became joyful thanksgiving.

During the winter Christian again was away from home much of the time, butchering for the neighbors. If the distance was more than a few miles and he had several days' work at the same place, he did not even come home for the night. Susanna was glad that Mr. Reimer was living with them so that she was not alone with the children, and also happy that they did not live far from Uncle and Aunt Leisy.

But Mr. Reimer was not good help on the farm, and did not really enjoy living on one. He had been a baker in Germany and knew nothing about handling horses. In fact, he was afraid of them. When spring came he decided to go to St. Louis and work in a bakery. Even though they had enjoyed his friendship, and Christian now had to find another farm helper, neither Susanna nor Christian were really unhappy to see him go.

Christian had become increasingly interested and active in the work of the Summerfield church. One Sunday as they were driving home from morning services he confided to Susanna, "Recently I have been feeling more and more often that God is calling me to preach. I felt it very strongly again today. I have even selected the text for my ordination sermon if I am chosen. It is 1 Peter 5: 6 and 11: 'Humble yourself therefore under the mighty hand of God, that he may exalt you in due time; To him be glory and dominion forever and ever. Amen.' But I will not say anything about this to anyone but you. I want to be sure that it is God's will and not just my idea."

He looked so humble and sounded so earnestly sincere that tears came into Susanna's eyes.

"We will pray that God's will be done," she told him

softly as she reached over and put her hand on his.

Susanna was expecting another baby, and during a cold spell late in the spring she caught a severe cold. She felt so miserable that it was hard to drag herself through the days, taking care of the two little boys, cooking something for her family to eat, washing their clothes by hand, doing the mending, and keeping her house tidy.

When another son was born in April, 1862, she missed Barbara's help and companionship, but fortunately a thirteen-year-old cousin, Anna, was willing to come and stay with the family and help with the housework.

Little Henry was a big, husky baby, but soon after his birth Susanna realized that something was wrong. He developed severe cramps, his whole body grew as stiff as a board, he had no voice when he cried, and he would not nurse. Anna helped Susanna give him a warm bath and a thorough massage each day, and gradually he got better. When the cramps stopped and finally even his hands lost their stiffness, Susanna's days were again filled with silent prayers of happy thanksgiving.

Christian took time out that spring for something more important to him than getting his field work done.

The second General Conference had been held at Wadsworth, Ohio, so Christian had not been able to attend it. But when the third one was held in the Summerfield church in 1863 he enthusiastically attended every meeting.

When he came home on the second evening, Susanna could tell as soon as he walked into the house that something special had happened.

"You must have had an interesting meeting," she remarked. "What special decisions did the delegates make today?"

"Two important things were decided," Christian told her enthusiastically. "The decision was made to establish a Mennonite school and to send Pastor Hege as a traveling minister to create interest in the project as well as in mission work. But they had a hard time deciding where to have the school. They talked back and forth and couldn't come to any agreement. I wasn't sitting with the delegates since I wasn't one, but at one point when there was a pause in the discussion, I felt led to ask, 'May those who are not delegates also speak to the question?'

"The chairman, John Oberholtzer, gave a friendly assent, so I told them, 'The school should be built in the center of the Mennonite population. Today Ohio is the center; in another ten years Kansas may be. But for now I propose Wadsworth, Ohio.' That started the discussion again, and can you believe it, they quickly agreed on Wadsworth!"

That summer Susanna was so busy that even with Anna's help she sometimes wondered how long she could keep up her schedule of early to work in the morning, late to bed at night, and hurry, hurry, hurry to get everything done during the day.

Christian had bought a harvester, much like the one that Father had owned in Iowa. It cut grain like a haying machine and as the grain fell onto a platform a man raked it off and other workers bound it into bundles. Then two men arranged the bundles into shocks. That meant that Susanna and Anna had to feed nine or ten men three meals a day. And in Illinois it was customary to serve a lunch at 10 o'clock in the morning and 2:30 in the afternoon in the fields.

This lunch consisted of baked rolls or cookies and a drink. Many of the farmers served beer, others served coffee. Christian didn't want to serve an alcoholic beverage, and he thought that coffee was too much work. So he bought small bottles like soda pop bottles and filled them with cider to take out to the field.

Feeding the men was an exhausting schedule for Susanna and Anna. By the time they got back to the house after taking the morning lunch out to the men they had to hurry to prepare the noon meal. And by the time the dishes were washed after that meal and the little boys settled for their afternoon naps, the afternoon lunch had to be fixed. After that came the evening chores—milking the cows, feeding the hogs and chickens, gathering the eggs, then hurrying to have the evening meal ready.

104

Susanna was happy when harvest time was over. But, unfortunately, she found that life didn't become much easier then. Christian and David Lehman again ran Uncle Leisy's threshing machine, going from farm to farm most of the fall. Susanna and Anna did not have to prepare the noon meals for the men nor bring out lunch to the fields, but they did have to do the chores.

Then, even before the threshing was completely over, something happened that kept Christian away from home for a number of weeks.

The young Summerfield minister, Daniel Hege, had been asked to go on a preaching mission through all the eastern states to awaken interest in the school to be established at Wadsworth, Ohio. When he came back to Summerfield he reported to the congregation.

Busy as he was with his farm work, Christian took time out to go to each meeting where Hege spoke about his work.

"Pastor Hege had done his work wonderfully well," Christian told Susanna after the first evening. "Not only had he secured several thousand dollars worth of pledges for the school at Wadsworth, but he seems to have awakened a sense of unity and zeal for missions among the Mennonite people where he has been. And now, as he tells about his experience he's giving us a better understanding and love for these brethren in the East whom we've never had a chance to meet and whom we'll probably never learn to know personally."

"I'm glad things worked out so well for him," Susanna said. "And I'm sure his wife is happy to have him back home. She told me that she gave up their home to live with the Vogts because she didn't want to stay alone with the children while her husband was gone. From the way she talked, she didn't expect him home so soon."

"Oh, he's not at home to stay yet," Christian said. "In fact, as soon as he has rested a few days, he plans to go to Iowa to speak to the churches there. They are very much interested in what he has to report about the contacts he made."

Not long after that Mr. Vogt came to talk to Christian.

"Pastor Hege came back from Iowa," he said. "But he

became ill with typhoid fever while he was in St. Louis, and now he is very sick. In fact, he has been delirious part of the time. He needs someone to take care of him, and he told me that he would like very much to have you be his nurse."

Susanna knew that Christian had farm work that needed to be done, but she was not surprised to have him say, "I'm very sorry to hear that Daniel is sick, but I'll feel honored to be his nurse. I'll give our hired man some instructions about the work that needs to be done here on the farm, and what doesn't get done, just won't get done."

It was only a few weeks later that Christian came home to report, "Daniel passed away last night."

"Oh no!" Susanna exclaimed, shaking her head. "I didn't realize he was that sick! "Yes, he was a very sick man!" Christian told her. "And he knew that he was. He was ready to die and had set his earthy affairs in order. Toward the last he was often delirious, but there were also unforgettable times when his mind was clear and he spoke to me about his great faith. He will be greatly missed, but his influence will linger for a long time!"

"What about his wife and children?" Susanna wanted to know. "What will they do now?"

"She plans to go back to Ohio where her parents live," Christian told her. "And I have invited her and the two youngest children to stay with us until her father comes after her. The oldest boy wants to continue staying at the Michael Wuerpens with their son, who is a good friend."

"Oh, I'll be happy to have them here," Susanna exclaimed. "After all, she's your cousin. And since Mr. Reimer is no longer staying with us they can have the room where he lived.

CHAPTER 18

Susanna sat quietly on a chair, holding baby Henry in her arms. She had never felt so completely depressed and discouraged and frightened in her life. Her wonderland had betrayed her! Christian had been drafted into the United States army!

She thought about what Christian's father had sacrificed to keep his sons from having to take military training in Germany. He had given up his lovely, large farm in Bavaria to come to America to live in a small log house on land that was mainly woods with a few acres of unbroken prairie. In a way he had even sacrificed his life, because if he had stayed in Bavaria the skillful doctors there could probably have prevented his death at such a young age.

And now Christian, a mature man with a family of children, and also his younger brother Valentine had been drafted. They were not only to train for military service, but to actually take part in the warfare.

Susanna had been aware that the country was at war. She had even heard that so many men had fallen in battle that there were fewer and fewer young men who were enlisting to serve as soldiers, so the government had resorted to the draft. But the fact that her Christian might be drafted had never entered her mind!

What was she to do? How would she manage, alone with the three little boys? She didn't even have a home she could call her own, and only debts as property. If Christian had to go into the army and could no longer farm the land, she might even have to leave the home where they were now living!

There was one ray of hope. Mr. Buckinger, who had married a member of the Mennonite church, worked in the coal mine in Summerfield. He told Christian about two young men who worked in the mine who would be willing to go into the army as paid substitutes.

That was where Christian was now. He and Valentine had gone to the mines to talk to the two young men. What if someone else who was drafted had already asked them and they were no longer available?

"I shouldn't even think about that," she told herself. But she couldn't put the thought out of her mind, and her tears began to flow again.

When she heard the house door open, she knew it must be Christian. She felt herself shaking. But when she looked at Christian's face she could see that he had good news. He was smiling happily.

"I have a substitute," he told Susanna, giving her a happy hug. "And so does Valentine. Mine is a young German by the name of Remigius Mantele, and Valentine's is a Mr. King. Tomorrow we'll take the two to Alton. We'll check in there, then our substitutes will go to camp and we will be able to come home.

Susanna spent the rest of the evening saying silent "thank you" prayers. She slept better that night than she had since Christian had received his draft summons.

Christian left home early the next morning to pick up his brother Valentine and meet Mr. Mantele and Mr. King at the mine to take them to Alton. By late afternoon Christian was at home again. The next day he went to work in the field as he had been doing. Life for Susanna settled back into its familiar pattern.

That fall was a happy one after all, especially during the time that Father and Mother Ruth came from Iowa to visit for several months.

Those were relaxing days for Susanna, and her little boys

received more attention than they had ever had in their lives.

But the following spring brought a change that was not so pleasant.

Mr. Reimer died. His brother in Germany sold the farm on which Christian and Susanna were living to a rich man in Germany. This man's brother, with a good friend, came to Summerfield to take over the farm. Since they stayed in the Krehbiel's home while they made definite plans about moving there, Susanna's life was certainly not made any easier.

Their fourth son, Jacob, was born on May 7. Susanna was happy that Christian's mother came to stay for several weeks. When she left and Susanna was alone with the children again, she found herself dreading the summer months when she would have to get ready to move from their home.

"We have to move," she kept thinking. "But where will we go?"

Even Christian had no easy answer to that question. He was still half owner of the farm where they had lived when they first came to Illinois. But going there to live with the Lehmans again, now that the size of both of their families had grown, was out of the question.

Busy as he was with his farm work, Christian took time to drive around in the Summerfield area looking for a farm to rent. But he could not find any. The farms that were for sale were too high priced for him to consider buying. He came home each time with a discouraged look on his face.

"I'll find something before we have to move," he reassured Susanna, but she could tell that he was not sure of that himself.

Then one evening he came home with good news.

"I found out that the section of unbroken prairie about five miles from here is for sale at a very reasonable price. It's the only unbroken prairie left around Summerfield. I'd have the work of breaking the prairie before I could plant anything there, but it would be good, fertile soil. I can't afford to buy the whole section myself, of course, but I think I can find some others who are interested in buying part of it."

"My brother John wants to move here to Summerfield,"

Susanna reminded him. "I think he would probably be interested in buying part of this land."

"And the Vogt brothers have been thinking of buying farms of their own," Christian added. "They might be interested. So I think everything will work out all right."

Within a few days Christian was able to make definite plans for buying the section of land. When he talked to David Lehman about it, David suggested they sell the farm on which he was living. Then each of them could use the money to buy one hundred acres of prairie land. The Vogt brothers were interested in buying sixty acres each. Susanna's brother John answered Christian's letter by writing that he would like to have sixty acres.

John came from Iowa to make definite plans for his part of the property. When he was ready to go home, he talked Susanna and Barbara into going with him to visit in Iowa.

"This will be the first time in four years that I've been back there," Susanna told Christian. "That's right. I think you should certainly go," he replied.

Susanna thoroughly enjoyed visiting Father and Mother and her brothers and sisters. It was satisfying to worship in the church that had once meant so much to her, and to visit with friends and relatives whom she had not seen for a number of years.

But as she got onto the boat to go back to Illinois she thought about the day she and Christian had left Iowa to go to Summerfield. "At that time I was very reluctant to go," she told Barbara. "But now I can hardly wait to get home."

When work on the new farm began, Susanna found herself even busier than she had been before. Her brothers, Henry and Jakob, and a neighbor boy, Christ Beutler, walked the five miles to the new farm every morning to break the prairie, dig a well, and build fences. Three carpenters—Susanna's brother David and Christian's cousins, David Krehbiel and August Lehman—also went to work there. All of these young men stayed at the Krehbiel home. They had a stove in a small building they had erected on the new farm, so they could make coffee and keep food warm. Susanna cooked breakfast for them and prepared a lunch each morning for them to take along. In the evening she did not have to milk the cows, but she did have to take care of the hogs because the workers came home so late. After that she had to cook supper for all of them.

That fall, Christian was "drafted" to do work that was different from serving in the United States army, but which would take a lot of his time from then on.

After the death of Daniel Hege, the other two ministers, Mr. Hirschler and John Schmidt, pushed for the election of someone to help them. When the election was held, Christian and his brother Valentine had the most votes. When the lot was drawn, it fell on Christian.

The next Sunday morning, with tears of happiness in her eyes, Susanna listened to Christian preach his acceptance sermon. He based it on the Bible verses he had quoted to her a number of years before, 1 Peter 5:6 and 11, "To him be glory and dominion forever and ever." She knew how much this call to the ministry meant to Christian.

This was the beginning of a new era in Susanna's life. Happy as she was that Christian had achieved his wish to become a minister, she found that their life at times was so busy that she wondered how long she could cope.

The work on the buildings on the new farm progressed slowly. Christian drove back and forth daily, bringing the things the carpenters would need. In the fall he plowed and seeded at the new farm in the daytime, then at night set up the corn shocks at the place where they were still living.

That winter smallpox struck the community. In late January a friend, Mr. Risser, died from the disease. Christian was asked to be in charge of the funeral. Susanna bundled up little eight-month-old Jacob and drove along with him. When they got to the house they found that no one was there who could lay the corpse into the coffin, so Christian had to do it. When he got home, he left his coat outdoors, but not the rest of his clothes.

In a few days Christian became sick. Smallpox broke out on his body, but not on his face. It did not take long before he felt better. However, a few days later little Jacob became sick with a high fever. Soon the pox appeared over his whole body. His eyes were completely shut. His entire face was crusted over, his tongue was swollen and bleeding, and his lips were so bad that blood flowed from them when he tried to nurse at Susanna's breast.

That was only the beginning. Soon the illness made the rounds of the house. Everyone except Susanna was affected. At one time all ten of the other people in the house were bedfast, and Susanna was hard pressed to try to take care of all of them.

By March the new house was far enough finished that Christian and Susanna decided to move in. It was a small house, but they felt happy and fortunate that they now had a home that was their own. There was still much that needed to be done. They needed to plant trees, to start a garden, and to buy a number of furnishings for the house.

There were also debts to be paid, but at least they could live in their own house. With God's help these other things could be taken care of and they would still be able to buy the necessary furniture and other things they needed.

The Krehbiel's first daughter, Katie, was born on April 10, 1866.

"Now we finally have a little girl," Susanna happily told Christian. The older brothers were delighted with their little sister.

The spring was rainy. Soon the boys all came down with a cold fever, the ague, and were very sick. After harvest Susanna also became sick, but she developed a fever. She was sick with it off and on throughout the fall and winter. The boys' fever also returned again and again, so there was always someone who was sick. Sometimes there were two or three sick people at a time. Susanna never had to tell her little sons to be quiet. They were always sitting still when they were not lying down.

The Mennonite periodical, *Christliche Volksblatt,* announced that the school building at Wadsworth, Ohio, was to be dedicated just prior to the fourth General Conference, which was to be held in Wadsworth, October 15-19, 1866.

There was no question about whether or not Christian would attend the dedication and conference.

Several months before these events, he received a letter from John Oberholzer, the conference president, asking him to preach the first sermon in the school at the opening session of the conference. "I suppose I was asked to do this because I was the one who suggested Wadsworth as the place to build the school," Christian remarked after he had read the letter.

Susanna agreed that this was probably so. "I wish I could attend the conference and hear you preach that sermon," she said wistfully. She knew, of course, that women did not attend such conferences. Anyway, it was out of the question for both her and Christian to be away from home at the same time.

When Christian got home from the conference, he was enthusiastic about the school building. "It's a stately building," he said, "but modest in appearance. And I think it has been planned very suitably to its purpose. It is three stories high, has a flat roof, in the center of which rises the little tower containing the bell. The upper story is arranged for a dormitory. The other stories are divided into rooms and halls as required for school purposes. The kitchen, dining hall, and storage rooms are in the basement. In general, I think the building is nicely arranged without much display or unnecessary ornamentation."

About his sermon he had little to say.

"I think it went all right," he told Susanna when she asked him about it. "I had prayed a lot about what I should say. When I got up to preach, I just turned myself over to God's leading. I think everything went all right."

Later, she had a chance to read the article about the conference in the *Friedensbote,* a German religious periodical. Susanna decided that Christian had been too modest about what he had told her.

A.B. Shelly, the editor, had written an article about Christian's sermon. He began by describing Christian as "a young and powerful man of robust appearance, positive yet modest bearing, who wears a heavy beard." He ended with the words, "This powerful address by Christian Krehbiel, which I have only imperfectly touched at a few points, stirred me to the depth of my soul. I may well say I have never heard a more beautiful sermon."

When she called Christian's attention to the article, Christian read it. Then he said quietly, "I told you that I turned myself over to God's leading."

Soon after Christian came back from the conference, he and Susanna had another important decision to make.

The year before this, in 1865, Susanna's father had bought a farm on the edge of Summerfield to which he and Susanna's mother had moved in March. Susanna's younger brothers were farming it, but preferred working for others, so Father decided to turn the farm over to Christian.

One of Christian's brothers was glad to buy the farm where Christian and Susanna were living, so Christian willingly sold it and bought Father Ruth's farm. Since Father and Mother Ruth wanted to live in the house with Susanna and Christian and their family, Christian had to add extra rooms to the house. In the process he got further into debt. He was willing to do that to be able to live so much closer to the church where he was adding more and more responsibilities. And the children were much nearer to better schools where both German and English were taught.

After the house was rebuilt, Susanna's parents had two rooms downstairs and one room upstairs, and also a separate pantry. The Krehbiels had two rooms downstairs in addition to a kitchen and a small room for farmhands. There were four rooms upstairs. Most of them were quite small, with just room enough for a bed and some space to turn around in.

The additions to the house were finished by February 1867. The Krehbiels moved to their new home soon after that. When Susanna's father died on March 6, both Susanna and her mother were glad that they were living together, especially after Mother began to suffer with painful neuralgia soon after that. Christian was also happy that they had made the move. He was especially glad to be living so close to the church.

Because Susanna's mother lived with them now and

114

some of the children were old enough that they were helpers instead of needing to be taken care of, life for Susanna became easier and more pleasant in many ways. But her work did not really become any lighter.

Christian had accepted even more responsibility at the church than he had before. When John Schmidt, the elder, wanted an assistant, Christian's brother Jacob was chosen. But he had a problem with failing eyesight and soon asked that another man be chosen in his place. So another election was held. This time it was Christian who was elected.

At Christian's insistence, Father Schmidt continued his role as elder, with Christian as his assistant. But soon Father Schmidt was turning more and more responsibilities over to Christian. By the time Father Schmidt died, Christian was able to carry on the work with confidence. Christian's brother Jacob was chosen at that time to share the services with Christian.

In January 1868 another son was born. Christian and Susanna decided to name him Daniel. They gave him the middle name of Remigius, in honor of Remigius Mantele who had made it possible for Christian to avoid serving in the army during the Civil War.

In addition to his responsibilities in the local church, Christian had accepted an even more time-consuming responsibility. The General Conference had appointed him as a field secretary to the extent that his work in Summerfield would permit. His first assignment was to go to Franklin, Iowa, to persuade the members of the Zion church to release their teacher, Christian Schowalter, to answer the call of the Wadsworth school to be a teacher and house father there.

This was only the beginning. In addition to his work for the General Conference he had also accepted the assignment as home missionary of the Western District Conference (later called the Middle Conference). This involved traveling to various isolated communities in Missouri and other states where small groups of Mennonites had settled. He was also elected president of the Foreign Mission Board.

All of these responsibilities left him little time for his family or his farm work. After being away from home on an assignment he would come home for a few days, check on the work that the hired men had done, and give them suggestions for more work. He would also read his mail and write any necessary letters in response.

There would, of course, be a few hours each day for his family, but to Susanna this never seemed enough. She did not complain because she knew how important his work for the church was to Christian. But she often thought back longingly to the first year of their marriage when there were long evening hours for the two of them alone in their little stone house.

In some ways life was easier for Susanna than it had been in the past. She was fortunate to find capable, congenial girls to help her with the housework and the gardening. The older boys were growing up and assuming more responsibility for the chickens and the barnyard chores. And Christian had bought her a small sewing machine so she no longer had to sew her dresses, the children's clothes, and Christian's shirts and underwear by hand.

The machine was screwed to the table and then run by hand. Susanna never did have to turn the wheel. The older boys enjoyed doing that. But they liked to run the machine so fast that Susanna sometimes had trouble stopping as quickly as she needed to.

Summerfield was quite a large town at that time. There were two hotels, a shoemaker, a tailor, many coal miners, and at least four saloons. Many people in the town needed to buy milk. Christian decided that meeting this need would be a good source of income for his family.

At first the older boys carried the buckets full of milk to the customers before they went to school. After school they picked up the empty buckets. But the demand for milk quickly outran the supply. So Christian bought more cows and a pony and buggy for the boys to haul the milk.

All of this meant more work for Susanna. She seldom had to help with the milking, which was done by hired hands. But she did have to fill the milk buckets and oversee the whole procedure whenever Christian was not at home.

116

This business enlarged until they were milking thirteen cows. The milk sold for five cents a quart, and they took in about $800 a year.

There were other things that kept Susanna and her sons busy. In addition to the small garden near the house, Christian had prepared another garden, about an acre large, which he plowed instead of spaded. Still, this garden needed a great deal of hard work before things could be planted there.

In this garden Susanna raised many vegetables, more than she could use for her family. So in the mornings she packed some into the milk wagon and found a good market for them. After she had put up a barrel of sauerkraut and many sour beans and pickles and other vegetables for her own family, she still sold eleven bushels of beans for canning and several dollars worth of seed beans.

Happy as she was for the extra income, Susanna was glad when the fall season brought a temporary rest from the gardening. In September 1869 another little son was born. This time Susanna chose the name.

"I think it is time we named one of our sons after his father," she told Christian with a teasing smile. Christian did not argue with her, so this little son was named Christian.

CHAPTER 19

Eighteen seventy-one brought several important changes to Susanna's life. For one thing she did not have to cook for as many farm workers as she had in previous years. Farm machinery had improved so much that not as many men were needed for harvesting the grain. And the older boys, twelve-year-old David, eleven-year-old John, and nine-year-old Jacob, were big enough to help in the fields.

In June a second little girl was born. This time it was Christian's turn to suggest a name. "I think we should name our little daughter after her mother," he said. Susanna was happy to agree.

Susanna still did not have a sewing machine, and the little hand machine had been used so much that it was no longer working. So everything that she needed for the little newcomer had to be made by hand. Fortunately she had Christine Risser, a capable, willing young woman, to help her with the work.

Interest in the West was spreading at this time. Many people from the eastern states came through Summerfield on their way to Missouri, either to visit there or to establish a new home. Since most of them knew Christian because of his visits in their churches for the General Conference, many of them stopped at the Krehbiel home before going on.

Remembering his own experiences when he was traveling for the General Conference, Christian insisted that they be invited to stay in the Krehbiel home until they traveled on.

Fortunately, Susanna had a few more rooms available for these visitors than she would have had some years earlier.

Mrs. Lehman, Susanna's sister Barbara's mother-in-law, had passed away several years before. After a suitable period of mourning, Mr. Lehman had asked Susanna's mother to marry him. After the wedding she had moved into the Lehman home. This meant that the rooms Mother had used were available to Christian and Susanna's family. But even so, the older boys often had to give up their beds and sleep on the kitchen floor or on the grass outdoors when guests came to visit.

Some of the young men in Summerfield had also become interested in the western states. Farms in the part of Illinois where they were living were very expensive. Interest rates were high. The income from a small acreage was so small that it was impossible to get out of debt.

Five young men from Summerfield decided to make a trip by wagon to the West in the fall to check on things. They were Christian's brother John, who was married to Susanna's sister Katharine; Dan Lehman, J.B. Schmidt, Abraham Stauffer, and Susanna's brother Gerhard.

Katharine found it hard to be left alone on the farm with her three little children, the youngest of whom was only six months old. Susanna worried about her. She invited Katharine to stay in the Krehbiel home while John was gone, but Katharine felt she should not leave the farm without anyone living there to look after things.

When the men came back to Summerfield they stopped first at Christian and Susanna's house to tell them that they had traveled home from Kansas through Nebraska and Iowa. John Krehbiel had become sick on the way, so they had left him in Iowa with his sisters and brothers until he would be well enough to travel again. Then he would come home by himself either by boat or by train. Christian immediately drove out to the farm to tell Katharine, and to check on things there.

Two days later Susanna and her mother had gone to town. They were in the little store that Jacob Krehbiel had in one room of his house when a messenger boy came with a telegram. Jacob had trouble with his eyesight, so he handed the paper to Susanna to read.

The telegram had been sent by Christian's brother Daniel from Iowa. The words Susanna saw on the paper were such a shock that she had difficulty reading them out loud.

John had died. His brother Daniel wanted to know what he should do, what plans he should make for the funeral.

Susanna and her mother rushed home and told Christian, who fortunately was not away on a trip. He immediately harnessed some horses to a wagon and took Susanna out to Katharine and John's home.

Katharine opened the door before Christian had a chance to knock. When she saw only Susanna and Christian standing there, the smile on her face was quickly replaced by a frightened, questioning look.

"She recognized our wagon, but she thought we would be bringing John home," Susanna guessed. "And now she can tell from our faces that we don't have good news."

"John is worse?" she asked as Susanna and Christian walked into the house.

Susanna put her arm around Katharine. Christian said quietly, "We received a telegram from Daniel saying that he had died."

"I've been afraid this might happen," Katharine said in a strained voice. "But I kept hoping and praying that it wouldn't."

She slipped out of Susanna's arms and sat down on the nearest chair, with her head bowed and her hands clasped tightly together.

After a few minutes she looked at Christian and asked, "Can I go to Iowa to see him and help make plans for his funeral?"

"We'll talk about that tomorrow," Christian told her gently. "We don't know any details. If only the weather weren't so bad. For now, why don't you get together some clothing and other things you will need if you do go, and come with us for the night."

Susanna helped Katharine gather together the things she would need for herself and the children. Christian carried

120

them out to the wagon. Then he took out some bedding and fixed a place where the children could lie down in the wagon, and Susanna and Katharine could sit beside them.

"That will be enough for tonight," he said. "But as soon as we can, we'll come and get the rest of your things and bring them to town. You can't continue living out here by yourself with the children."

As soon as they got back to Summerfield Christian contacted the Lehmans, and David and Barbara came to the Krehbiel home.

After discussing the matter, they decided that Christian would go to Iowa for the funeral. David would go with him so he would not have to go alone. Katharine decided to stay in Summerfield.

"There is nothing I can do to help John now," she said, fighting back tears. "With the weather so cold, I don't want to take the children with me. But they would be very unhappy if I went and left them here. I'll just remember John as he kissed me good-bye when he left for Missouri."

After the men got back from Iowa, Christian and Susanna took Katharine out to her farm and helped her pack her things. They moved her furniture into the rooms that had been Mother's before she married Mr. Lehman.

Christian took over the work on Katharine's farm. He had a public sale for the cows, horses, and chickens. In the summer he harvested the wheat. Then he sold the machinery and later he sold the land. All of the debts were taken care of and Katharine had money for necessary expenses.

People continued to stop at the Krehbiel home on their way to the western states. But they were not all from the eastern states. A number of them came from Prussia and Russia.

Christian had received a letter from Cornelius Jansen, the Prussian consul in Berdyansk, Russia. The letter had been written to Daniel Hege, and sent to an address in Pennsylvania. It had come into the hands of John Oberholzer, who sent it to Christian because he knew that Daniel Hege was no longer living.

From this letter and others, as well as from what he

read in the newspapers, Christian knew that these were troublesome times in Germany, France, and Russia. There had been revolutionary social and political changes. In the process, the German province of Prussia had withdrawn the Mennonites' exemption from military service. A short time later, Russia, which had attracted Mennonite settlers by guaranteeing them freedom from military service indefinitely, likewise retracted its promise. Many of the Mennonites in Prussia and Russia were thinking about migrating to America.

However, the first· Prussian and Russian visitors to Summerfield did not come because of this problem.

In 1872 three young men stopped in Summerfield and came to the Krehbiel home. Two of them, Bernard Warkentin and Dick Wiebe, were both from well-to-do families in Russia. They were simply stopping in Summerfield as part of their travels to "see the world." The third man, Mr. Baehr, a slightly older man, was serving as a guide for the other two.

Since the three could speak no English, they were ready to finance the travel expenses of anyone in Summerfield who would accompany them on their trips to various places in the United States. A number of young men from the area happily took advantage of the opportunity.

The three men had come back to Summerfield in the fall. They were making plans to return home when news came that Warkentin's fiancee had died in Russia.

For Warkentin the news was emotionally devastating! "That it should happen while I was away!" he kept saying. "She seemed in good health when I left. I was planning to get home before Christmas, and was hoping to be married soon after that. Now I don't even want to go back. I'll just stay here until I can reconcile myself a little to what has happened."

So the other two went back to Russia, and Warkentin stayed in Summerfield. He visited in the Krehbiel home frequently, and Susanna was always happy to have him come. He was so well educated and polite that conversation with him was always interesting. He soon became a close friend of the family. When Susanna gave birth to another son on March 17, 1873, she and Christian decided to name him Bernard after this special friend.

Christian was now busy from morning until night, and often far into the night, answering the letters from leaders of groups in Europe who wanted to come to the United States. He had continued his correspondence with Cornelius Jansen. He was also exchanging letters with Leonhard Sudermann, the leader of a large Mennonite congregation in Berdyansk, Russia, giving them information about the various possibilities of having groups of Mennonites settle in the United States.

There was also the problem of what to do about those who could not afford to pay for their passage or to buy land after they got to the United States. An aid committee to help the immigrants was formed in Pennsylvania. In order to do their share in giving practical help to these immigrants, the Mennonite church in Summerfield also formed a committee called the Mennonite Board of Guardians. This committee dealt with the problem of providing financial aid to those who needed it. Christian was named chairman, Bernard Warkentin was president, David Goerz was secretary, and John Funk was treasurer.

Word must have gotten to land agents for the Atchinson, Topeka, and Santa Fe Railroad Company that a Russian Mennonite was staying in Summerfield, and that a large delegation from Russia was expected in 1873 to explore lands which, if found satisfactory, might attract large numbers of immigrants. The railroad owned large tracts of land in Texas, Kansas, and other states. Representatives of other railroad companies who owned land in the western states, began knocking at the Krehbiels' door. One of these, a Texan, took Bernard Warkentin and J.E. Schmidt and some others from the Summerfield Mennonite Church on an inspection tour of Texas. Although the men thought the soil there was good, they felt the climate would be too warm for the Mennonites from Russia.

Warkentin had sent detailed reports praising the situation in Kansas to the Prussian and Russian congregations. He fully expected the delegates who came to America to select him as a guide, if not as their leader. But the delegation representing various Russian and Prussian Mennonite congregations who came to America in 1873 at first did not come to

Summerfield. From Pennsylvania they headed for Canada, which offered closed settlements in Manitoba and exemption from military service.

Warkentin stayed in touch with them by mail. After the deputation had made its tour of Canada, some of the members decided to visit parts of the United States also. Warkentin met them and accompanied them through Minnesota, Nebraska, Iowa, and Missouri to Summerfield.

Three members of the deputation got to Summerfield ahead of the others. This time it was the Missouri, Kansas, and Texas Railroad that found out about these European visitors and sent a representative to Summerfield to praise their company's land and offer free transportation for inspection.

The representative, Mr. Goodenow, did not speak or understand German, so he needed interpreters. Since the members of the Summerfield Mennonite Church had become interested in finding new lands for themselves also, they delegated John A. Ruth and Christian to go with the group.

Because of the many trips Christian had made for the General Conference, Susanna should have become accustomed to his being away from home. But even though she now had her sister Katharine living with her, she still found herself feeling apprehensive and lonely at the thought of Christian being gone for such a long period of time, especially in the spring, one of the busiest times of the year.

Their oldest son, David, seemed to feel the same way. "I'd like to see Father off at the station," he told Susanna. "I don't like to have him going away from home again."

Christian, who had overheard the conversation said, "I'd like very much to have you see me off, son. I don't like to be away from home right now either, but I feel like I have to fulfill my obligations to the church, too."

Life settled into its usual routine after Christian was gone. Susanna, with Katharine's help, did the housework and looked after the younger children. The hired men, with some help from the older boys in the evening, did the field work and the barnyard chores.

Then, early in May, David came home from school in

the morning, not long after he had gone to school.

"I feel sick, and the teacher told me to go home," he explained.

Susanna put her hand on his forehead. "You don't have a fever," she told him. "So you probably have the ague again."

She gave him the regular medicine. By evening he seemed to feel better. In the morning he said he would like radishes for breakfast, so Susanna went out to the garden to get some. David started to follow her out, then suddenly he turned around without saying anything. When Susanna got back into the house, she saw that he was lying unconscious across his bed.

In a panic, Susanna telephoned the Summerfield doctor. To her relief he was able to come at once. After he had examined David, he asked to have another doctor come for consultation. Susanna sent for their old German doctor at nearby Lebanon.

He, too, came without delay. After he examined David, he motioned for Susanna to follow him out of the room.

"Where is Christian?" he asked her.

"I don't know exactly where he is right now," Susanna had to admit. "He went with a group to look at land in Kansas. I have a copy of his itinerary, but I don't know exactly where he will be on any given day. He couldn't say that for sure."

"How long will he be gone?" was the next question. Again Susanna had to say that she didn't know exactly how long.

"I don't like to have to tell you this," the doctor said quietly. "But if it is at all possible to telegraph Christian, do it at once. Tell him to come home as soon as possible if he wants to see David again while he's alive."

As soon as the doctor was gone, Susanna got out the list of places where Christian had said they would be going. She tried to decide where he might be.

"Help me, God," she prayed silently. Then she told Katharine, "I think I'll send the telegram to Parsons. Christian wrote that they would be in that area for several days. But I don't even know where to go to send the telegram."

"Why don't you call our brother David?" Katharine suggested. "He'll probably know how to do it and where to go."

David drove to St. Louis and sent the telegram. On Sunday Susanna found her prayers answered. Christian called from St. Louis to say that he was there. Since no trains ran from there to Summerfield on Sunday, brother David drove to St. Louis in the buggy to get him.

David's convulsions had temporarily stopped when Christian got home, so the two could talk to each other.

"I'm so glad you could come home," David told his father. "I was afraid you wouldn't find out about my being so very sick."

"It's almost like a miracle that I did," Christian told him. "A small group of us had visited with the depot agent at the train station in Parsons for a little while before going to our hotel, so he knew my name was Krehbiel. He also knew where we would be staying for the night. I had just walked into the hotel when I was told that there was a call for me from the depot agent. He told me that soon after I had left he noticed the name 'Krehbiel' coming over the telegraph wire. He watched and caught the message, 'David very sick; come home at once.' So instead of going to bed, I checked out of the hotel and took the next train home."

Even with Christian at home, the next weeks were very difficult ones for Susanna. David needed nursing care day and night because he was in constant pain and could do nothing by himself. Since the spine near the brain was affected, he was often delirious. The doctors did all they knew to do, setting leeches on his forehead and using ice packs, but nothing helped.

On June 9, 1873, he passed away. Susanna was torn between relief that David's suffering was over and deep grief at the loss of this special son, her firstborn, who had always been so loving and helpful.

For weeks Susanna had to fight against a deep feeling of hopelessness and depression. The rest of the summer turned out to be so busy that she often wanted to throw up her hands and resign from the demands of her life.

That summer a number of representatives of various

churches in Russia, as well as some Prussians, several families and even single people, came to Summerfield. They rented a house in which to live until others from their group arrived. There were others who came only for a week or so to get information and advice. These always stayed in the Krehbiel home.

This was a difficult time for Susanna and her sister Katharine, who was still living in the Krehbiel home with her children. Much of the time the older Krehbiel children had to sleep outdoors or crowd together in the hired help's room next to the kitchen so the guests would have a place to sleep. Then there was the problem of what to cook for the meals since there was not much in the way of groceries to be had in the Summerfield store.

These guests did not bother Susanna as much as the important men from the steamship companies, and the railroad and land agents. All of them stayed in the Krehbiel home when they came to talk about prospective land buyers with Christian. The men would sit in the dining room to discuss their plans and problems. The baby lay in the cradle there, and all traffic had to pass through the room when going from the kitchen to the cellar or another room.

That summer and fall when Christian wasn't discussing matters with these land agents, or away on a trip with some group interested in buying land, he was writing letters by day and far into the night, trying to acquaint the various churches with the problems of the immigrants. At the same time he was working on a plan for the Summerfield and Iowa congregations to move to Kansas.

In January 1884, a group of thirty men, most of them from Summerfield but some from Iowa, went with Christian to look at land in Kansas. They had a private railroad car to sleep in at night after having looked at the land during the day. At Halstead the car was put on a side track to serve as a hotel during the time they were there.

When Christian got back from the trip he reported to Susanna. "All of us bought land. To get a full section of land I had to go far north of Halstead to the country between Newton and McPherson. I chose Section 27, and I had to pay

127

$4 an acre. Christian Voran, Christian Hirschler, and my brother Daniel bought sections next to mine. In the middle, where the four sections joined, we laid out a town site which we named Christian, Kansas. Daniel is building a store on his land. I made arrangements to have a church built on the corner of my land. But I also selected the east half of Section 1, just east of Halstead, to exchange for the parcel of land that I had reserved for me in Marion County."

A number of letters were waiting for Christian. One of them was a call for him to come to Berne, Indiana, to install S.F. Sprunger as minister.

"So you have to leave right away again?" Susanna sighed.

Christian stood quietly for a few minutes looking at her. Then he said gently, "I know it's hard for you to have me away from home so often. Why don't you come along with me on this trip. It will be good for you to get away from home for a little while. Barbara Eyman is a good maid. She and the older boys will help Katharine look after things here while we're gone."

Susanna could hardly believe what she was hearing! This was something that she had thought would never happen. She had been tied down at home for so many years. Even when all of the others had attended the St. Louis Fair, she had not been able to go along. When there was no small baby to keep her at home, she had not felt like going anywhere because she was pregnant again. She had come to accept that this was the way that life was for her.

"But what about Bernard?" she asked. "He's still nursing, so I can't go without him."

"We'll have to take him along, too, of course," Christian assured her. "Trains are much more comfortable than they used to be, so it wouldn't be a big problem to have him with us."

Susanna thoroughly enjoyed the train ride. She was thrilled with the warm reception that Christian and she received from the people at Berne. And by the time they were ready to leave she felt that she had added a number of good friends to her life.

Susanna still did not like the idea of moving to Kansas, a

place that seemed so unsettled to her. So when Christian had to go there again on some business in May, he talked her into going with him so that she could see for herself what it was like.

Susanna had to take Bernard along again. This time he became quite sick from the motion of the train. The ride the first day was anything but pleasant.

But soon after they left Topeka, a porter came and transferred them from the car in which they were riding to the private car of Mr. Touselin, the land agent. There the seats were more comfortable and there was much less noise. While Christian and Mr. Touselin discussed business, Susanna lulled Bernard to sleep, and then got some rest herself.

In Halstead, Christian and Susanna found Peter Wiebe at work building his house, and Bernard Warkentin, with his partner, Albright, building the mill. The Sweese Hotel, where Susanna and Christian spent the night, was packed because there was a large group of men in town who were building a bridge over the river next to the mill.

The next day Christian borrowed a farm wagon and two horses from Peter Wiebe. He and Susanna left Halstead, driving back and forth on the prairie all day. Christian had many orders to buy land for the people who could not come on the first expedition to Kansas, but who wanted to buy land. He had the plats, and he hunted for the land that had not yet been bought.

They had taken a lunch with them, which they ate at noon. By sunset they came to the home of their good friends, the Rupps, who had come to Kansas in April. They had a small one-room shanty for their three families of twelve persons—Father and Mother Rupp, two sons and their wives and children, and a son-in-law, H. Dester. Crowded as these families were, they heartily welcomed Susanna and Christian.

On Sunday morning, with rain pouring down outside, they had a church service in the home. Afterwards they had an enjoyable visit, and lunch and supper. Christian and Susanna spent the night there. By Monday morning the rain had stopped, so Christian and Susanna drove back to Halstead in clear, sunny weather. Christian drove crisscross across the prairie, looking for land that had not yet been chosen.

On Tuesday they drove south of Halstead. The land agent had designated land for a school in each of the four townships set aside for the Summerfield group. Christian was to select this land also.

Then they inspected the land that Christian had bought, the east half of the section just east of Halstead. Susanna did not like it; it seemed too sandy to her. But it had been bought, so she didn't say anything about that.

They stayed at Halstead until Christian had taken care of everything that he had been asked to do. Ten days after they had left Summerfield, they were back at home again. And even though Susanna still did not really want to move to Kansas, she now knew what it was like, and was better able to make plans for the move.

Chapter 20

Soon after they got back to Summerfield, Christian again became so involved with the emigrants from Europe that he had little time for his family. Susanna found herself busy again with visitors in the Krehbiel home!

Reverend Wilhelm Ewert, with his wife and six children, came to Summerfield from Prussia. Mr. Ewert, a well-to-do, capable, generous man, had brought with him a number of poor Mennonite families from Poland. He had paid for their passage with his own money. He and his wife and the two youngest children, as well as Peter and Eva Bartel from the Polish group, stayed in the Krehbiel home. The others were placed in the homes of other members of the Summerfield church.

A few days after their arrival, Ewert discussed his plans with Christian. He was going to Kansas to buy a farm for himself and also eighty acres of land for each of the needy families that he had brought to America.

"That is very generous of you!" Christian told him. "But I would suggest that you retain the title to the land you buy for them and rent it to them on reasonable terms. Build a house and barn and other buildings that they will need, and see that they have the use of the machinery they will need. Then have them give you as the owner of the land a third of the crops and let them keep two thirds for themselves. In that way you can help them learn how to farm in Kansas and also how to manage their money."

Mr. Ewert agreed that this was a good idea. "That is what I'll do," he told Christian. "The expense will be the same for me, but I'll have better control of the situation."

In the spring Mr. Ewert and most of the families he had brought to Summerfield left for Kansas, where they settled near Hillsboro and founded the Brudertal congregation. But the Bartels decided to stay in Summerfield with the Krehbiels.

Many other Mennonites from Europe came to the United States from Europe that year. There were two groups of immigrants that made separate journeys to America from the large Alexanderwohl congregation in Russia.

Elder Jacob Buller headed the first group. He first led his people to Nebraska, but was not received there as he had expected to be. He lost no time in accepting the proposition for settling in Kansas that J.B. Schmidt of the Santa Fe Railroad sent to him. His large group decided on land about twenty miles northeast of Newton, where they founded the New Alexanderwohl Mennonite Church.

The second group, under the leadership of Dietrich Gaeddert, also came in 1874. Christian, as one of the members of the Board of Guardians at Summerfield, was notified when they left Russia. Later information was telegraphed to Christian that they would be going by way of the Ohio-Mississippi line to St. Louis.

The information even included the time when they would come through Summerfield. So the members of the Summerfield church decided to meet the train. During the brief stop they walked through the cars and passed out food and fruit to the surprised and delighted passengers.

Since the group had to change trains in St. Louis, Christian and several other members of the Summerfield church went along as interpreters. Susanna's brother David accompanied the travelers to Kansas City, where another change of trains had to be made.

The Board of Guardians had assumed that this second group from Alexanderwohl would settle near the first group. Christian found out later that they selected land about twenty-five miles west of the first group. There they founded the

Hoffnungsau Mennonite Church with Gaeddert as their elder.

Soon after that, another group came to Christian's attention. A number of Swiss-Volhynian Mennonites, whose elder was Jacob Stucky, came from Russian Poland under the contract of the Board of Guardians. Since the members of the Summerfield church had not taken all of the land reserved by the Santa Fe for them, Christian got permission from Mr. Touselin to offer it to these immigrants.

They accepted the offer and established the Hoffnungsfeld community between the land north of Halstead and Mr. Gaeddert's group farther to the north and west.

Quite a number of these Swiss-Volhynian Mennonites later went to South Dakota. They had hard going the first years and some of them came back to Kansas and founded a settlement near Pretty Prairie. All of them, after the first years, made out quite well.

When he became acquainted with them, Christian found out that the ancestors of many of these people had originally come from Switzerland. Some of the Krehbiels traced their ancestry back to the Primmerhof in the Palatinate, which was also the home of Christian's ancestors.

A number of other smaller Mennonite groups also came from Europe to Kansas in 1876 and 1877, settling near Newton, Brainerd, Whitewater, Elbing, and Hanston. Others settled in Nebraska, Minnesota, South Dakota, and Manitoba. But with these Christian was not really involved.

That fall Susanna was thankful that the Bartels were living in the Krehbiel home. Her sister Katharine came down with such severe rheumatism that she had to be in bed for months. She was almost helpless. Susanna was pregnant again, so without Eva Bartel's help she could not have managed to take care of Katharine in addition to doing all of the other work that needed to be done.

The baby, a little girl, whom they named Mariechen, was born on January 26, 1875. The weather was icy cold and there was no stove in Susanna and Christian's bedroom upstairs. So Christian moved Susanna and the baby downstairs into Katharine's room, where there was a stove. But on the seventh day the baby became sick, and the next day she died.

Susanna mourned the little one, but she thanked God that she herself felt well. She was able to be up a week after the birth, and could help Eva with the work and take care of Katharine. The work had really been too much for Eva. The older boys, and even Katie, who was still in school, had to help.

Christian's time was again completely taken up with the problems of immigrants from Europe. He had received a telegram from Warkentin saying, "One hundred families without food; send money and men to help."

When he got more information, Christian found out that the Aid Committee of Pennsylvania had paid the travel expenses of a large group of very poor people from Volhynia, a Polish section of Russia. These people had been turned over to the Santa Fe for the last part of the trip to Kansas. They had been dumped by the railroad in Florence, with only an empty store building for shelter. Now the care of the large group of wretched people was up to the Board of Guardians, who had not had any advance notice of their coming.

The Board of Guardians was not willing to drain their treasury for these immigrants who were really the responsibility of the Aid Committee of the Eastern States. So Christian again sat at his desk most of the day and far into the night writing letters and working out plans.

He asked David Goerz to depict the plight of these people in his publication, *Zur Heimat*. As a result collections were taken in many churches. The Board of Guardians was able to meet the most important needs of these unfortunate people without draining their treasury.

"So these people have food and a temporary place to stay," Christian said to Susanna. "But they need more than that! I've been told that there are a lot of young adults in the group who need a chance to work and earn some money. I'll see whether I can find some people here in Summerfield who would be willing to hire them. And I'll ask Goerz to mention the matter in *Zur Heimat*."

Christian did find jobs for twenty-four young people in Summerfield, and a number of other communities were willing to hire some of them. So Susanna's brother David went to Kansas to bring them to Illinois.

Two of these young people, twenty-year-old Heinrich Koehn and his sister, sixteen-year-old Helena, worked for the Krehbiels. They were good workers, but they spoke and understood only Low German, which Susanna neither spoke nor understood. So it was sometimes difficult for Susanna to communicate with them.

Since Christian was the one who had brought these young people to Summerfield, the whole group usually spent Sunday in the Krehbiel home. They were homesick for their families and also for the homes they had left in Europe. Some of them had received letters from their parents. They wanted Susanna to read the letters to them. Then they dictated letters for Susanna to write to send back to their families in Kansas.

The people for whom no employment was found had to stay in the abandoned store building in Florence, Kansas.

"We'll have to find some way to help these people get onto land so that they'll be able to take care of themselves," Christian said repeatedly. "There's some land left near Canton in McPherson County that was reserved for us Mennonites. But these people don't have any money with which to buy it."

In the weeks that followed, Christian again sat at his desk each day and far into the night trying to work out some plans to help these poor immigrants. He ended up with three plans, each of which would fit a different situation.

Plan 1. The railroad company is to allot to each family so desiring, forty acres of land in the vicinity of Canton, McPherson County, and is to make no demand for payment for at least five years. Financial aid to families taking up forty acres under this plan is to be given by the aid associations either in the form of outright gifts or loans where conditions warrant.

Plan 2. Any of the Summerfield group or other persons who have bought land in Kansas but have not yet occupied it, shall, if they can afford it, build a house on the land. They shall take in one of the stranded families as tenants, and supply the needed implements, cows, and draft animals

135

against a note. They shall pay the tenant $3 an acre for breaking the prairie, furnish seed for the first planting, permit the tenant to retain the entire first crop, and thereafter receive rent.

Plan 3. Any who already live on their land or who plan to move onto it this spring (1875) shall, in addition to their own house, build another on the property for one of the needy families. They shall supply it with foodstuffs, which the family itself is to prepare for use. In return this family shall work for the owner at an appropriate wage.

As its contribution to carrying out this program, the railroad company is to lay down in Halstead, freight prepaid, one carload of building material for each family that is located under any one of these three plans. The benefit of this prepaid freight is to go to such families as settle on forty acres under Plan 1, and to the owners of the land who take tenants under Plans 2 and 3.

It is proposed that all branches of Mennonites in America be informed of the plight of their stranded brothers and sisters in faith and urged to come to their aid, either with outright donations or with loans of money. The funds are to be administrated by a special body—the Kansas Aid Committee—representing both the Aid Committee and the Board of Guardians.

Christian discussed these suggestions with the members of both the Aid Committee of the Eastern States and the Board of Guardians of the General Conference. The program met with general approval and was adopted. So Christian began making plans to begin carrying it out.

Several families from the Summerfield church had gone to Kansas in the fall of 1874, but the first large group to go— the John Ruths, Dan Haurys, Valentine Krehbiels, Dettweilers, John Kuehnys, and John Lehmans left in March 1875.

Peter and Eva Bartel also went with the group. Christian had decided to have them settle on the land he had bought in McPherson County in Kansas when he and three friends had thought of founding the town of Christian, Kansas. He carried out some of his suggested plans by having a house built for them. He furnished them with horses, wagon, and other necessary equipment on credit.

The church members decided to establish a congregation in Halstead as soon as they got settled there. They held services in the schoolhouse until they could build a church. Christian's brother Valentine had been elected minister and elder, and Christian was asked to install him.

So Christian also went to Kansas at that time. He stopped in Topeka to get Mr. Touselin's acceptance of the railroad's involvement in the plans he had worked out for the immigrants settling in the Halstead area. Then, after he had finished his obligations in Halstead, he went to Florence to visit the immigrants living there.

What he found was even worse than he had expected. About a hundred families with children were living in an empty store building that was only about eighty feet by thirty feet. The place was drafty and cold, but without proper ventilation. There was very little food. What there was had to be prepared outside at the back of the building because there was no room for cooking facilities inside. And there were no facilities for bodily cleanliness, no privacy, and no fresh air.

After holding a worship service for these people, Christian presented his plans for a settlement program for the group. It was greeted with great enthusiasm. Christian and the rest of the Kansas Aid Committee began to implement the plans for settling them as a community near Canton.

With all of these obligations out of the way, Christian began to make plans for his family's move to Halstead. In the spring of 1877, he sent sixteen-year-old John to Kansas with a freight car filled with machinery, cattle, and fodder. He was to live with his Aunt Ruth. During the day he was to break the prairie on the Krehbiels' land. John wrote home regularly, so Susanna and Christian knew just what he was doing. He broke the prairie and planted a corn crop. Then when it had matured he harvested it. When that was finished he came back to Summerfield.

That winter Christian sold the Summerfield farm to Susanna's cousin David Ruth, with the understanding that the

Krehbiels would vacate the place by the following March.

In April 1878, both John and Henry went to Kansas, again with a carload of cattle, horses, and mules. Again they planted corn and wheat and had a good crop of each. In August, Christian went to Kansas again. This time he wanted to see about building a house on the Kansas farm. So when he and the boys were not working in the fields they were busy carpentering.

As soon as the barn was built they lived there, with a small room arranged as a kitchen. And before Christian went back to Summerfield they had a house finished far enough so the boys could live in it during the winter.

That fall was a busy one for Susanna. There was a good fruit crop in the orchard at Summerfield. Knowing that there was no orchard on their farm in Kansas, Susanna wanted to take along as much of the fruit as she could. Canning had been invented by that time, so Susanna, with the help of her sister Katharine and the older children, canned as many of the peaches as they could. They also made sweet pickles. The apples were picked during the week and piled into a wagon. Then on Saturday they worked with them, making vinegar from the early tart ones and drying or canning the others.

There was also a good grape crop, from which they made wine. They ended up with sixteen barrels of vinegar, three sugar barrels lined with heavy paper full of dried apples, seven barrels of wine, 300 quarts of apples, and one hundred gallons of apple butter.

On November 16, 1878, two weeks after Christian had come home and all of the work with the fruit was done, Susanna gave birth to twins. They were large, healthy children whom they named David Ernest and Edward Benjamin.

When the boys were a week old, Christian again had to leave home to attend a conference. As soon as he got back the final work of getting ready to move had to be finished. In February 1879, the Krehbiels held an auction of all the things they could not or did not want to take along. The other things had to be packed and loaded into the train cars. These cars were to be shipped so they would arrive in Halstead by the time the family did.

On March 16, nineteen years to the day after they had moved to Summerfield, Susanna, Christian and their family left the little town where they had experienced so much pleasure and so much sorrow.

When they got to Halstead, Bernard Warkentin met their train. He took Susanna and the smaller children to stay in the Warkentin home until the Krehbiel's house was completely finished. A few days later, as she stepped over the threshold of their new home with the prayer, "Our entrance be blessed," Susanna found herself feeling happy and content. If all of the family was together again under the same roof, what did it matter if the house seemed far too small for all the chests and trunks?

As soon as things were fairly well in order in the house, Susanna busied herself with planting the garden and orchard. She had brought along all kinds of shrubs and small fruit trees, and these had to be planted at once.

Christian had plowed the lot which was to be the garden in the fall, so Susanna could also plant the vegetable seeds. But to her dismay she soon discovered that the grasshoppers that had plagued Kansas in the previous summer had laid their eggs in the fresh earth. As a result, more grasshoppers came up than seeds. The grasshoppers lost no time in eating the tender shoots that did grow.

"If only I had a hen with a brood of young chicks," Susanna found herself thinking.

A few days later when J.L. Schowalter brought the Krehbiels a basket of eggs, she asked him for help. He brought her a hen with fifteen young chicks the next day. The grasshoppers quickly disappeared from the garden and orchard.

Out in the fields the grasshoppers were even worse. Christian and the boys used all sorts of extermination, but much of the corn was eaten up before they finally were able to get rid of the pests.

The wheat crop was good, and since Christian now had a binder, he didn't need as many helpers. The practice of carrying lunch to the fields was left behind in Summerfield, so Susanna did not have to be concerned with fixing lunch each day. The work in Kansas seemed much easier to Susanna, especially since there was no fruit to pick and take care of, and the garden was much smaller. Susanna sometimes worried about what she would do when she had used up the supply of fruit they had brought from Summerfield. But the children told her, "We'd rather not eat any more apples if we have to pick them up." And Susanna found herself agreeing with them.

In August there was an epidemic of measles. Both of the twins got them, but quickly recovered. Then, a short time later, on a Sunday, little David became very sick, and on Monday, August 19, he died. And Susanna found herself almost ill again, mourning her loss.

Although that first year in Kansas was easier than in Summerfield as far as the work was concerned, it certainly was not as far as finances were concerned.

The Krehbiels no longer had the income from the dairy, the orchard, or the large vegetable garden. There were no hogs to slaughter for meat or lard. The one cow they had brought along had been killed in the train car. And there were still improvements and additions that had to be made on the buildings.

So cash was very rare, and that first Christmas Susanna had no money to buy presents nor even a little candy. Neither did Christian.

"But I'll see if I can get some for you," he told Susanna, with a twinkle in his eye. "I'll go visit your mother."

He went to town and soon came back with five dollars. He took Susanna back to town to buy a small gift for each of the children. Susanna had brought along the Christmas tree decorations, and Christian found a nice little evergreen tree in the pasture. So their first Christmas in the new home turned out to be a happy one in spite of the scarcity of money.

CHAPTER 21

During the first years the Krehbiels lived at Halstead, interest in western states continued to increase. Many visitors came to see what things were like there. Since many of them knew Christian from his travels for the conference, it was natural that they would stop at the Krehbiel home. Susanna and Christian were always happy to see these acquaintances and invited them to stay in their home.

But even though Christian had built an addition to the house on the east side, and during the year had also fixed the cellar for a kitchen, there was even less room for guests in their Kansas house than they had had at Summerfield. So the boys had to sleep in the barn whenever guests stayed for the night. This wasn't so bad in the summer, but they got very cold there in the winter, and were always glad when the guests left.

Christian was no longer the conference minister, so he was not away from home as much as he had been. But he had responsibilities as one of the ministers of the Halstead church. He was also involved with the Indian mission in Oklahoma where missionary S.S. Haury, a member of the Halstead church, was working.

Christian made numerous trips to the mission. Susanna always worried whenever he left to go to what she thought of as uncivilized territory.

In the summer of 1884, Mr. Haury brought eighteen

young Indians to Halstead to help the Mennonite farmers with their work. His purpose was to bring these young Indians under Christian influence and to teach them how to work. A number of the fellows worked for the Krehbiels, so the whole group often gathered at their home on Sundays.

The next year Mr. Haury suggested that the Indians be sent to the Halstead Academy. When the Mission Board accepted the plan, Mr. Haury made a contract with the United States government, which agreed to pay traveling expenses and $160 per year for each student. So eighteen Indian boys lived in a house close to the academy where they went to school. A.S. Shelly was the housefather and Christian's brother Peter was the teacher. The second year G.A. Haury was both housefather and teacher. The second year a tract of land was rented where the boys could raise some vegetables. This meant they needed a team of horses and more tools. The following year some trouble arose because of the different abilities and requirements of the Indian boys and the other students at the academy. Plans were being made to move the academy buildings to a place north of Newton where a building had already been started for an institution that was to be called Bethel College. So it was decided to give up the Indian school.

Christian was disappointed at the failure of the project.

"If the school were transferred to a farm where these young Indians could learn to work as well as learn to read and write, I think everything would work out better," he told Susanna.

Susanna had long ago found out that when Christian had an idea he thought would work well, he lost no time in turning it into action. So she was not surprised when Christian told her, "I've offered to have the school moved to our farm at the cost of $100 from the government for each student. We'll have to keep our hired help to supervise the work the boys do in the fields and will need to hire some household help to supervise the girls at their work. And then, of course, a teacher for the academic part of their training."

Christian had a large house built adjoining the Krehbiel home. This house served both as school and dormitory for the

Indians. Even though the Indian boys would be helping with the farm work, the farmhands who had been doing the work had to be retained to supervise the work that the boys did. A teacher was hired. He also hired extra help in the house to supervise the work that the girls did.

The number of Indian children and young people in the school rose from eighteen to forty or fifty. In all, more than one hundred children came to the school. All of them attended the Halstead Mennonite Church on Sundays, and a number of them were baptized. The Krehbiel home was no longer simply a farm. Soon their place became known as Krehbieltown.

The Indian school at Krehbieltown ran successfully for ten years. Then the government decided to concentrate all the small Indian schools into larger government schools. So the Krehbieltown school had to close.

What was to be done with the building that had housed the school? Christian did not want it to stand empty or to tear it down.

During these years family life had continued to change for the Krehbiels. Three more sons had been added to the family after they moved to Kansas: Benjamin on November 16, 1880, Paul on January 28, 1882, and Lucas on March 7, 1885. By now only the two youngest were still at home. However, the Krehbiels had taken two little girls whose mother had died into their home.

This gave Christian the answer to his question of what to do with the building in which the Indians had been living. Uncle Leisy had left $5,000 in his will for establishing an orphanage. Only the interest on the money was to be used each year. The churches at Halstead, Garden Township, and Moundridge were designated as the directors of the fund. The building where the Indians had lived would be an ideal place for young orphans to live until they were adopted into homes. Christian got in touch with the Children's Home Finding and Aid Society of Chicago. Through them the Krehbiels got as many children as they could handle. Over eighty children were adopted into families at Halstead and nearby towns, but there were always a number of them in the house at Krehbieltown.

EPILOGUE

Susanna sat on her chair. Her hands rested on the table in front of her. Her eyes watched Christian as he slept on a bed nearby. How peaceful and comfortable he looked. How peaceful and contented she felt!

Her thoughts went back to the first year of their marriage. They were living in the little stone house on Father's farm and both of them were working for Mother and Father. How contented she had felt then, especially during the long evenings when she and Christian had been alone together. First there had been just the two of them. Later, after David's birth, there were the three of them.

How often she had thought back to that year and wished that she could repeat it. She had often wished that she and Christian could experience that close companionship again. But they had never been able to do this in the years that followed. There had always been other people demanding their time, especially Christian's time.

Now, finally, in 1909, her wish had come true, although the circumstances were not what she would have wished for. On January 30, Christian had suffered a stroke from which he was recovering quickly. While he was recovering there was time for her and Christian to eat together alone and talk with each other as they had done during that first year of marriage, before so many others had begun to make their demands on their lives.

144

As she watched him, Christian opened his eyes, yawned, and sat up.

"Well, that was a good rest!" he said as he swung his feet off the bed and stood up. "I think I'll drive out to the Haurys with my buggy and ponies. There's something I want to discuss with Mr. Haury."

When he opened the door, he added, "That wind has certainly come up. And those clouds look as though we may have a storm. So I won't be gone long."

Susanna stood at the window and watched as Christian hitched his ponies to the buggy. Then she went into the kitchen to begin preparing their evening meal.

Looking out of the window some time later, she saw Christian drive up to the barn door. Just then the storm broke. A violent gust of wind lifted the door from its hinges and hurled it to the ground. The door knocked Christian down and landed on top of him.

The hired man and the two sons who were at home brought him into the house and laid him on his bed while Susanna called the doctor.

There seemed to be little that the doctor could do for Christian. Two days later, without ever having regained consciousness, Christian passed away. Susanna found herself overwhelmed with grief and loneliness. Even so, she often thanked God for having given her those last peaceful, enjoyable months.

After Christian's death their son Bernard added a room onto his house. Susanna went to live with him and his family. This home was located on the western part of the section of land where Susanna and Christian had lived their last thirty years together. From this room, which Susanna now considered her home, she made long visits to her other children. She enjoyed a leisurely life of relaxation for which she had never had time before.

In a full-page tribute to his mother in *Der Herold* of April 20, 1920, C.E. Krehbiel wrote that his mother was able to attend worship services on Palm Sunday, but suffered a heart attack during the first week of April. She died the evening of April 19, 1920.

Funeral services were held in the First Mennonite Church of Halstead, Kansas, on Sunday afternoon, April 25, with Rev. J.E. Amstutz, in charge. Rev. Gustav Harder spoke in German and Rev. J.H. Langenwalter in English. The choir sang, "O Love That Will Not Let Me Go." Her grandsons carried her to her grave.

Had she lived three more days, Susanna would have experienced that love on this earth for eighty years.